7/12

DAYNA LORENTZ

NO SAFETY

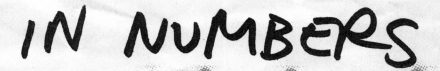

IN NUMBERS

Dial Books
AN IMPRINT OF PENGUIN GROUP (USA) INC.

DIAL BOOKS

An imprint of Penguin Group (USA) Inc.

PUBLISHED BY THE PENGUIN GROUP

Penguin Group (USA) Inc., 375 Hudson Street, New York, NY 10014, U.S.A. * Penguin Group (Canada), 90 Eglinton Avenue East, Suite 700, Toronto, Ontario, Canada M4P 2Y3 (a division of Pearson Penguin Canada Inc.) * Penguin Books Ltd, 80 Strand, London WC2R 0RL, England * Penguin Ireland, 25 St. Stephen's Green, Dublin 2, Ireland (a division of Penguin Books Ltd) * Penguin Group (Australia), 250 Camberwell Road, Camberwell, Victoria 3124, Australia (a division of Pearson Australia Group Pty Ltd) * Penguin Books India Pvt Ltd, 11 Community Centre, Panchsheel Park, New Delhi—110 017, India * Penguin Group (NZ), 67 Apollo Drive, Rosedale, Auckland 0632, New Zealand (a division of Pearson New Zealand Ltd) * Penguin Books (South Africa) (Pty) Ltd, 24 Sturdee Avenue, Rosebank, Johannesburg 2196, South Africa * Penguin Books Ltd, Registered Offices: 80 Strand, London WC2R 0RL, England

Library of Congress Cataloging-in-Publication Data
Lorentz, Dayna.
No safety in numbers / by Dayna Lorentz.
p. cm.
Summary: Teens Shay, Marco, Lexi, and Ryan, quarantined in a shopping mall when a biological bomb goes off in an air duct, learn that in an emergency people change, and not always for the better, as many become sick and supplies run low.
ISBN 978-0-8037-3873-7 (hardback) [1. Interpersonal relations—Fiction. 2. Survival—Fiction. 3. Quarantine—Fiction. 4. Biological warfare—Fiction. 5. Shopping malls—Fiction.] I. Title.
PZ7.L8814No 2012
[Fic]—dc23   2011051630

Designed by Jason Henry * Text set in Melior
Printed in the U.S.A.
1 3 5 7 9 10 8 6 4 2

For Evelyn

NO SAFETY IN NUMBERS

DAY
ONE
·SATURDAY·

MARCO

You know it's a bad day when you pull into the
parking garage at work and someone tries to run
you over. The car swerved toward Marco as he
pedaled down the entrance ramp. He wheeled into the
bumper of a parked car to avoid getting hit.

What kind of jerk is drunk and tooling around the
mall's underground lot at ten o'clock in the morning?

Then Marco recognized the car.

The driver was definitely a jerk, but most likely not
drunk. It was Mike Richter's BMW.

Marco had clipped the door of Mike's Beamer with his
bike pedal on Tuesday. He'd left a tiny scratch—a scratch
you would hardly notice if you were looking for it. Mike
had noticed. And had somehow, through the hissed ru-
mors of that nest of vipers called West Nyack High School,
figured out who did it.

The Beamer squealed to a stop, then Mike gunned it
in reverse, barreling down the aisle back toward Marco.

Was Mike trying to scare him or really run him over? From the relative speed of the car and the slightly weaving pattern of its course, there was a distinct possibility that in the process of driving like an asshole Mike might just accomplish both.

Marco hefted his bike and tried to squeeze between the nearest two cars, but Mike was thirty feet away and closing. Marco dropped the bike and ran for cover.

As he crossed to the next aisle, Marco heard his bike clatter to the ground. The Beamer's engine roared behind him. Then the crunch and scream of metal being crushed and dragged across the pavement echoed off the concrete walls. *Crap.*

It had taken Marco an entire summer of wiping down tables at the Grill'n'Shake to save enough for that bike— not that rich asshats like Mike understood such things. Now he'd be back riding the bus with the drunks and the bag ladies.

The Beamer screeched to a halt.

"Whoa, dude. I think you dinged the handlebars." Marco knew that voice: Drew Bonner, Mike's partner in terror. So it was two-on-one.

Marco knew Mike had it in for him—hard to miss the "You're dead, Taco" scrawled across his locker on Friday— but what he hadn't realized was that anyone at school knew he worked at the mall. Years of abuse had trained Marco in the tactics of survival, which boiled down to this: If every time someone spoke to you, you fired back some sarcastic, screw-you response, people tended to leave you alone. This method had served him well; now in his junior year, Marco was practically invisible to his peers. But not completely, as he was now aware.

The engine screamed—Mike was straining the belts. Marco's feet slapped the pavement as he booked it for the central pavilion: a small glassed-in room with the escalators up to the first-floor courtyard. From there, it was a quick jog around the central fountain to the elevators up to the third floor (multiplex theater, giant bookstore, bowling alley, ice-skating rink, and sit-down restaurants, including the Grill'n'Shake). No way Richter would chase him all the way up there.

But Mike cut the M3 down the aisle right next to the pavilion, squealing to a halt beside the doors.

"Come out, come out, wherever you are!" Mike shouted across the parking garage. There were already tons of people at the mall, meaning more than enough cars for Marco to hide behind, but alas, no helpful Samaritan or witness to his execution.

Marco leaned against the door of a green SUV and considered his options. He could run out the garage's exit and try to haul ass for the doors to the JCPenney. But that would mean spending at least five minutes on the road unprotected. Plenty of time for Mike to run him down.

Gravel crunched under the car's wheels: Mike was on the move.

"Where'd the Mexican mallrat go?" Drew yelled.

I've never even been to Mexico, you douche. Marco's grandparents were Costa Rican, and he'd inherited their black hair and olive skin.

"We'll sniff him out," Mike said.

Marco needed a better hiding place. As a busboy in a chain restaurant, he was intimately familiar with the bowels of the Shops at Stonecliff, the megamall under which he was currently trapped. He could book it for the utility hallway, then take the freight elevator. But that would mean fumbling in his wallet for the card key, and Marco's pockets were jammed with keys, bike lock, ghetto burner phone (who needed a decent phone when the only caller was your mom?), and iPod (link to his stake in the EVE-verse, controlled at home from his Alienware gaming laptop—cost: one year's wages). With Mike trolling the aisles, he didn't have that kind of time.

There was a light on by the Dumpsters. The door to the HVAC closet had to be open; it was the only possible source of light. Some guy must have been doing mainte-nance. For once, a lucky break.

The heating, ventilation, and air-conditioning system—HVAC for short—was housed in its own little bunker right next to the trash Dumpsters. It had no windows and only one door. If he could get in without Mike seeing him, he was safe for sure.

Marco crept around to the back bumper of the SUV. Crawling between the cars all the way down the aisle was an option, but the pavement was vile, and anyway, once he stood up, Mike would spot him. Marco figured Mike would have no qualms about smashing into a parked car and crushing Marco's legs, and he had no interest in end-ing up in a wheelchair over a scratched paint job.

Up and over it is. Springing onto the sedan's trunk, Marco began leaping from car to car, hood to trunk to hatchback to hood.

"He's over there!" Drew screamed.

Brakes squealed. Gears shifted. Marco had seconds to get back under cover. He hopped off a hood and hid behind a minivan. Then he dashed across the aisle, around a concrete pillar, and sprinted for the HVAC bunker.

Not only was the door to the HVAC room unlocked, but the gate in the chain-link fence that surrounded the giant machines inside hung open as well. Alas, he didn't have time to linger on why such a blessing had been bestowed on his sorry ass—he wasn't going to look a gift hiding-place in the mouth. He snapped off the light, carefully closed the chain-link gate behind him, and slunk into the thrumming dark of the HVAC cave.

The HVAC machines themselves were the size of small cars. Four of them sat in a row, each a giant block of metal with pipes like veins running into and out of them. At the end nearest Marco, two-foot-wide ventilation shafts protruded from each machine, running up into the mall to recirculate the temperature-controlled air.

Marco skulked between the whirring, vibrating metal shafts. Every few seconds, one of the giant fans inside the machines spun up, blowing the hair from his forehead in a single, soaked flap. Sweat poured down his face. Panels on the far ends of the machines blinked with little LED lights, flashing toxic orange and green across his skin.

The door creaked open. Marco slipped between two shafts and held still in the dark against the smooth side of an HVAC machine.

"You see him?" Mike called from outside.

Drew paused—Marco guessed he was peering around in the shadows. *Let him not see me, let them move on . . .*

"Nah," Drew said finally. "It's too dark, and I'm definitely not crawling into that rathole."

The door slammed closed.

Marco spit the air from his lungs in a single whoosh of breath. He flopped to the floor and held his head. He'd survived this encounter, but tomorrow? Or Monday at West Nyack Hellhole? Perhaps he should take a bus up to visit his sister, Frida, at Skidmore for a week and let Mike find a new target. Worst case, his oldest sister, Gaby, was in law school. She could sue Mike's rich-ass family for wrongful death.

He got up and turned on the light. The floor was disgusting. A thin layer of black slime coated the entire slab of concrete. He had to get up to work. He didn't want to lose this job, especially now that he needed a new bike. He brushed what muck he could from his jeans.

Then he noticed the second set of footprints.

"Is someone else in here?" he called. Perhaps there was a maintenance man after all.

The machine next to him clicked on with a blast of air. Marco nearly jumped out of his skin.

He followed the footprints around the machine. Nothing. The footprints stopped, then turned and went back out to the gate. It must have been the maintenance guy; he probably forgot to relock the fence.

Marco pushed the gate open. The bottom bar of the fence hit something—a chain. And a lock. A broken lock.

A maintenance guy wouldn't have cut the lock.

Marco shuffled back to where the footprints ended. He squinted, peered into the shadows. The wall of the

machine was smooth, interrupted in places by pipes jut-
ting out of the metal case and coiling back along its top.
Farther down was one of the blinking LED panels. It was
just like the other machines. Then a red light flashed.
None of the other machines had a red light.

Stepping back, Marco noticed that the light was attached to a small black box on one of the ventilation
shafts, just above his head. Nowhere near a panel. The
box had two bubble-like cylinders sticking out of its sides.
The box started to beep.

That can't be good.

Marco pulled out his cell phone and dialed 911.

LEXI

I f Mom is going to be on the phone the whole time," Lexi said, slumping in the backseat, "I don't see why Darren couldn't come."

Her father (one Arthur Ross) eased the Volvo into the parking space. "This is a family day. She won't be on the phone the whole time," he said. "Anyway, I thought you and Darren were cybernetically connected."

Lexi closed the game she'd been playing on her phone. "Not yet," she said. "But we're working on it."

Mom (the Senator Dorothy "Dotty" Ross) held up a finger. "John, I don't care if we have to move the committee meeting, but you set up that face-to-face with the governor." With her free hand she mimicked a yapping mouth.

Whatever. If her phone call was really some boring yackfest, why was the Senator on her cell instead of paying attention to her FAMILY? Especially when it was the

Senator's idea to drag everyone out on a Saturday afternoon to the godforsaken CommerceDome for a movie and
lunch at the fake-Chinese restaurant (the Senator's favorite, not Lexi's). A movie that the Senator would probably
end up missing because of the stupid call (it'd happened
before).

"Okay, John," Dotty said. "Sounds good." She lowered
the phone. "We're here!"

"You noticed," Lexi mumbled.

Her father gave her a *be nice* look. As if the Senator
cared whether her fourteen-year-old daughter was happy
with her. It's not like Lexi could vote.

The Senator craned her head around the headrest. She
looked like she was about to say something. Lexi braced
herself. Then the phone rang.

Dotty sat straight, opened her door, and answered the
phone.

The Senator couldn't even be bothered to ream her out.
That was how far down Lexi was on the priority list. Even
on "Family Day."

She got out of the car and followed her parents into
the mall.

Dad was carrying a bag. Why would he carry a shopping bag *into* a mall? *A gift?* Yes, that had to be it. A peace
offering. They totally owed her after forcing her to go to
Irvington Country Day, the prep school from hell, instead
of letting her attend public school like a normal person,
like Darren.

On the escalator, she stuck a finger into the bag and
caught a glimpse of the box. *No freaking way!* It was a

drawing tablet—had to be, judging by the size of the box. Plus, she'd been dropping hints that her old one was fritzing.

"No peeking," her dad said, tugging the paper from her grasp. Then he nudged her with his elbow. "We got the good one."

Visions of CG fairies danced in her head. "The professional?" It was a struggle to keep from yanking the bag from his hands.

Arthur stepped off on the third floor and tapped Dotty's arm. "Tell her, hon," he said.

Dotty walked a step away, pointed to the phone. *(LIKE WE HADN'T NOTICED!)*

Arthur shrugged. "You can open it," he said to Lexi, handing her the bag. He walked up to the hostess stand at Chopsticky Buns. "Three for lunch."

The hostess showed them to a booth and Lexi slid into the seat opposite her dad. Dotty was still standing by the entrance, blathering away into the phone.

"Dare I ask why you're giving me a five-hundred-dollar piece of computer equipment?" Lexi was going to make them say they were sorry for this whole private school nightmare. She wanted to hear that word: *Sorry.*

"Can't a father give his little girl—"

"I'm taller than you," Lexi said, nudging her dad's leg under the table. She'd inherited her mother's height, but not the willowy frame—she'd developed the obnoxious boobs and butt that bulged on her grandmother. One of the least thrilling hellos she got at Irvington: "What's up with that badonkadonk?" hollered up the stairwell.

Arthur snuffled a laugh and rubbed his shin. "Fine,"

he said. "Can't a father give his all-grown-up, high-school-attending, honest-to-god teenaged daughter a gift without getting the fifth degree?"

"Well, maybe."

The Senator sat next to Arthur. "Sorry!" she said, all blustery like she couldn't believe she'd been disturbed by a phone call. "So, you like the tablet thing?" The Senator was not into computers the way Lexi and her dad were.

"It's great," Lexi mumbled, sliding the package back into its bag. She raised her eyebrows at Dotty. "What's your excuse for giving it to me?"

Dotty's smile wilted at the corners. For a moment, Lexi regretted her sarcastic attack. Then the Senator drew herself up and took a deep breath in. "We get that you don't like the new school," she said. "But skipping class? Really, Lex?"

So that was it. Not regret over having ripped her out of public school to enroll her in a fancy, rich-kid prison. Not concern over the fact that she sat alone every lunch period staring out the perfect little framed windowpanes at the flame-colored leaves or that all the other kids at Irvington had been there forever and were all friends and totally ignored her. No, this "Family Day" was dedicated to rooting out what dysfunction had led Lexi to skip one freaking period (gym—who even needed gym?) to work in the computer lab on her movie. The drawing tablet was Dad's attempt at sugar to help Mom's medicine go down.

"*Class* seems like a strong term," Lexi said, dragging the bag off the table and into her lap. "It was gym. I didn't feel like playing volleyball-in-my-face."

"Is this a new thing for you?" Dotty said, leaning back

into the shiny, red fake leather of the booth. "Should we expect weekly reports of your delinquency as punishment for sending you to one of the top ten private schools in the country?"

"I didn't ask to go there," Lexi said. "I was perfectly happy in public school."

"Time-out!" Dad said, waving his arms between them over the table. "In your corners for at least ten seconds."

He winked at Lexi and she couldn't help but smile. She had the best dad in the universe. He almost made up for the fact that Dotty had become a Mom-strosity.

At first, the whole politics thing was fun. Mom was home all the time—the house was her campaign head-quarters. Lexi and Dad created the campaign website, programming while Dotty wrote the content. Mom would read them passages at the dinner table and they'd all help hone the prose. The website was the reason Lexi got into computer animation. It felt like the campaign was some-thing they were doing as a family.

Even once Mom was elected, she still tried to carve some private time out of her public life: There was the public Senator and the private Dotty. But then Dotty be-came the most senior senator on the Investigations and Government Operations Committee and now, three years later, there was really just the Senator. When Lexi saw brief glimpses of Dotty, it was usually to point out that her outfit didn't match or she really needed some new friends—"Not some online buddy to play Minecraft with, but a real friend in the real world."

Like it was that easy. Like Lexi could just flip a switch

and suddenly be friends with the snobby kids at Irvington. What was wrong with online friends, anyway? Lexi had almost three hundred friends on Facebook, and fifty people followed her Twitter feed, which was devoted to tips on computer animation techniques. And she had at least one real friend: Darren. They'd been inseparable since the release of the original Xbox—they met on the checkout line at the store and were instant partners in Halo decimation. At this point, they could wreck any punk who tried to challenge them. If she'd stayed in public school with Darren and their old computer geek crew, she'd have friends. It was Dotty's fault that she was reduced to a completely online existence.

The Senator flipped through messages on her phone. Dad sat silent in the corner, as if keeping watch to make sure the time-out was obeyed. The waitress came to their table and slapped some menus down.

"Welcome to Chopsticky Buns," she said in a drone. The paper lantern dangling low over the table threw unfortunate shadows across her pale face. "Can I get you something to drink?"

She glanced up from her pad and scanned the table. Her gaze lingered on them for just a beat too long before returning to the paper. It was something most people wouldn't even catch, a tick, nothing. But Lexi always noticed. Always felt those sidelong glances. Always knew that when people looked at her family they were trying to place them in the picture. A preppy and power-suited black family living in Westchester? And who's the kid with the boobs? What is *she* doing at Irvington Country Day?

"Chicken with broccoli as usual?" Arthur said, tapping Lexi lightly with a menu.

Lexi put her napkin in her lap. "Yeah, sure," she said. The waitress left with their order.

"They're going to change the name of that dish to 'The Alexandra Ross,'" he said, smirking.

"At this point, they could change the name of this restaurant to Ross's Kitchen and I wouldn't be surprised."

The Senator put down her phone. "Now we have to criticize my cooking?"

"She wasn't criticizing your cooking," Arthur said.

"Like you ever cook," Lexi muttered.

Dotty slumped back into the booth. "Okay, I surrender," she said, sliding her fingers over her hair. "You win, Lex. If you don't want to stay at Irvington at the end of the semester, you can transfer back to public school. Deal?"

She held her hand out like they had just struck some corporate bargain, negotiated a complicated budget proposal—like they were strangers. Maybe, at this point, they were.

Lexi slapped her mother's hand. "Deal."

"Good," Dotty said, sitting straight again. (*Problem solved! On to the next task! Busybusybusy . . .*) "Now, where's my egg roll?"

Arthur reached across the table and squeezed Lexi's arm. He gave her a *you okay?* look: raised eyebrows, slight smile. Lexi shrugged. It wasn't his fault the Senator had lost all interest in her daughter.

The Senator's cell phone rang again. Dotty sighed— Lexi thought she saw something of her mother there, an exhaustion with the job as opposed to her delinquent daughter—and then picked up the phone. "It's Frank," she said. "I should take this."

"Like you'd ever ignore a call," Lexi snarled.

Dotty glanced at Lexi with large, sad eyes. "Really, Lex? Have I fallen so far?" She swallowed, then hit TALK. "What's up?"

The waitress appeared with their appetizers.

Dotty picked up her egg roll. "I'm actually there." Her expression changed. She put the egg roll down. "They found what?"

Dotty got up from the table and walked out of the restaurant.

Lexi could not believe what she had just witnessed. Her mother lived for Chopsticky Buns' egg rolls. She could not fathom what information could have caused the Senator to leave an egg roll uneaten.

Arthur looked as stunned as Lexi. His mouth hung slightly open and his eyes lingered on where Dotty's back had hustled past the hostess station. "Let me see what's going on," he said, sliding out of the booth. He shuffled between the tables, leaving Lexi alone with the blue flame of the pu-pu platter as her only company.

Her phone buzzed. *Not my only company*, she thought, smiling. It was Darren, as she'd guessed. She slid her finger across the touchscreen and saw the text.

Movie any good?

Still at lunch, Lexi wrote back.

You could always just wait with me for the illegal download.

Lexi snorted a chuckle. *Careful or I'll sic my mom's committee on you.*

I await The Man's imminent arrival. There's the black van now. Oh, and here's the dude in sunglasses and a suit to drag me off to Guantanamo.

Swift kick to the groin should finish him off.

Darren texted a frowny face. *Never joke about kicks to the groin.*

Dad sat back down in the booth. "Darren, I presume?"

Lexi typed a quick *TTFN* and put her phone back in her bag. "Who else do I have to talk to?"

"Could be there are some decent kids at Irvington, you know." He picked up a shrimp stick and held it over the flames.

"Don't you start in on me too," Lexi said, lifting a chicken wing. "Is the Senator coming back?"

"You mean your *mother*?" Arthur said, frowning.

"Yes," Lexi muttered, rolling her eyes and dropping her head back.

"I know you can't see it, but she's trying," he said, lowering his food. "This job is pulling her in a million different directions."

Lexi poked a discarded foodstick into the blue flames and watched it flare up, then disintegrate. "So what's the crisis this time?"

Arthur tipped his head as if he were going to try to prod their conversation back to the Senator's lame attempts at parenting, but then picked up another shrimp. "Some situation in the parking garage the mall manager needs help with. She said to eat without her."

As usual . . .

■　■　■

When they finished their meal, the Senator still hadn't surfaced, so Arthur suggested they check out the new graphics cards at the Apple Store. As if Lexi would ever say no to that.

She made a beeline for the new desktops. The store had preloaded a professional-grade graphic design program on the floor model. Lexi decided to take it for a test drive. She hacked the Internet firewalls, accessed her iCloud, and opened her movie project.

"Wow," said a vaguely familiar voice. "That looks amazing."

Lexi turned around. The voice belonged to a girl from Irvington. A popular girl. She stood there with her perfect red curls in her perfect little outfit, her pissed-off-looking perfect friend behind her. *Ginger Franklin*. Lexi remembered the name from roll call in fourth period Ancient History. She'd thought it funny that a "ginger" was named Ginger and texted Darren about it. He'd texted back that her parents must have been getting back at her for being a miserable baby.

Ginger pointed at the computer screen. "I saw you working on that at school. It's amazing."

"Thanks," Lexi said. She clicked the mouse and the window collapsed.

"Don't be shy," Ginger said. "You're really good. Like, Pixar good."

Lexi's brain grasped for an explanation of why Ginger was talking to her. She felt like she'd been ambushed, like some guy with a camera was going to jump out from behind a curtain and scream, "You've been punked!"

"Can you show me how to do that?" Ginger asked.

"Weren't we going to Abercrombie?" the pissed-off friend groaned. Lexi suddenly recalled *her* name—Maddie Flynn. Maddie had (intentionally?) spiked a ball into Lexi's face during gym the other day. She flicked her wrist and glanced at her watch, as if her time were so important and not a second could be spared.

"Go on," Ginger said. "I'll meet you there."

Maddie snorted—at least Lexi could have sworn she heard a snort. "Fine," Maddie said, and stalked out of the store.

Ginger smiled at Lexi. "Maddie's kind of got a one-track brain," she said.

"You could say the same about me," Lexi said.

Ginger wrinkled her perfect nose. "You're funny," she said. "Alex, right?"

"Lexi," she replied. Then, after a heartbeat, she added, "Why are you talking to me?"

"Is that a problem?" Ginger asked, pulling a stool over. "Look, I don't mean to come off as a freak or anything, but I saw what you did in the lab at school. How do you do it?"

Lexi had never before met someone who felt comfortable just sitting next to complete strangers and asking them about their totally private, top-secret movie projects. Was this how one was supposed to make friends in that alternate universe known as Irvington Country Day? *No wonder I've spent the last month and a half alone . . .*

Ginger raised her perfectly plucked eyebrows and smiled encouragingly.

"It's not hard." Lexi turned back to the computer and opened a blank project.

Ginger flicked her hair out of her face and watched the screen as if Lexi were about to deliver crucial test-prep information. Not sure what else to do, Lexi showed her a few simple things with the graphics program.

It wasn't hard to impress Ginger; she seemed blown away by a stick figure walking across a white screen.

"That's amazing!" she said, eyes wide. "And you did it in, like, three seconds. Amazing."

Lexi felt a smile break out across her face. She knew her work was amazing. Compared with some of the amateur stuff on YouTube, her clips looked professional. But it was one thing to think it to herself and another algorithm entirely to have one of the most popular girls at her school utter the words.

"If you think that's cool, wait until I add a wireframe."

"Oh my god, let's do it." Ginger dragged her stool closer.

Lexi choked on a laugh. The girl was legitimately psyched about a computer program. Even Dad had never been this excited about one of Lexi's animation projects.

The mall's speaker system crackled to life, silencing the Muzak that had been droning quietly in the background.

"May I have your attention," the Senator's voice said. "There is currently a security situation being handled in the parking garage. We ask that you please remain calm and make your way to the nearest store. Remain inside the store. We will update you shortly."

Leave it to Dotty to turn some car alarm crisis into a "security situation."

"Guess Maddie will have to wait a little longer than she thought," Ginger said, glancing over her shoulder at the crowded corridor. Then she nudged Lexi's arm. "Let's get going on the frame-y whatnot."

Screw the Senator. *I have the coolest girl in ninth grade sitting beside me, waiting for me.*

Lexi turned back to the screen and began clicking through menus. She would show Ginger wireframing, how to add avars—she'd make Ginger a fully functional 3-D character. She'd make her a whole 3-D world.

Her phone buzzed in her pocket—*Darren.*

Ginger glanced in her purse. "Not mine," she said.

"It can wait," Lexi said, ignoring the text. "Watch this." And a new person emerged on the screen.

RYAN

Ten more minutes, and Ryan would have been out of Toxic, zombie makeup in hand. He would have been at Shep's Sporting Goods, maybe already halfway up the climbing wall. But no, the security situation had to shut down the mall and here he was, stuck with the emo kids between racks of studded collars, fake leather pants, and T-shirts with things like "Black Death European Tour" on them. Not a store Ryan would normally shop in.

But Ryan's brother Thad, the quarterback, had said the West Nyack High School varsity football team would go as zombies for Halloween practice before heading out to the usual party at Mike Richter's house. As the newest and youngest member of the varsity team, and younger brother of the QB, Ryan felt a lot of pressure to do everything right—no, not right. Better than right. On the field and off. Ryan owed everything he was to Thad, given their parents' inability to do anything besides lay into each other over money, a crap dinner, or nothing at all. He wanted to make his brother proud with the big stuff and the stupid, like this costume.

Having nothing else to do, Ryan flipped through the nearest rack, which was packed with flowing skirts in acid green, fuchsia, black. *Who would wear this stuff?*

"Do you mind?"

The rack had spoken.

Ryan stepped back. "Hello?"

Two hands appeared from inside the wall of material, separating two skirts and revealing the most stunning face Ryan had ever seen or even dreamed of. The face smiled.

"I'm only joking," she said. "But you did smack me in the eye with a string of beads."

The girl stepped out from between the skirts. She had rosy brown skin and huge, weird green eyes rimmed in black lashes, and this waterfall of black hair. She wore some strange, shiny golden cut-off top over a flowing, flowered see-through muumuu with skinny jeans and black boots. Thin gold chains with charms dangling from each circled her long neck, which featured a tattoo of a vine curling around it, ending at a flower that bloomed on her left cheek.

"I'm Shay," she said, sticking a hand out.

Ryan was pressed against a glass case full of silver skull rings.

"And you are?" she asked, arching a perfect black eyebrow.

"Ryan," he finally managed. He took her hand. Her skin was warm and smooth.

"It's the tattoo, right?" Shay said. It wasn't just the tattoo, but Ryan was happy to let her start with that.

"It's henna," Shay continued. "Like my parents would ever let me get a real tattoo. But that's the plus of living with your Indian grandmother. There's always lots of henna." Shay looked through the front windows of the store at the corridor. The only people visible were two mall security guards patrolling the other side of the hall. "Where'd everyone go?"

"Didn't you hear?" Ryan asked, still trying to get a hold of his heart rate. "The mall cops ordered us to stay in the store. Some security thing in the garage."

"Oh." The smile faded from Shay's face. "I should find Nani and Preet."

"Who and who?" Ryan asked.

"My grandmother and sister. I left them in Aéropostale. Preeti takes forever to pick out a pair of socks."

Ryan suddenly felt the need to keep Shay from moving. "We can't leave," he blurted out. "The mall cop said so."

"The mall cop?" she said, smiling. "I think I can face the wrath of the mall cop."

She reached into the rack and pulled out a book and her iPod. *So that's why she missed the announcement.* The book was a ratty thing; the yellowed pages curled and the cover was so faded, Ryan could barely make out the name.

"Tagore?" he asked, desperate to keep her there, even if it meant talking about a book. "Is that, like, foreign or something?"

"Or something," Shay said, smacking him lightly on

the arm with the book. "He's only the most famous Indian poet. He won the Nobel Prize."

"Oh." Ryan could not have felt like a bigger idiot. He'd maybe read one poem. Ever. And he thought maybe it was some kids' book thing about farts. "You reading it for school?"

"No," Shay said. "I'm reading it for me." She held his eyes for an intense moment. "Here." She handed the book to him. "You look like you need this more than I do."

He took the book from her, letting his fingers brush her skin. Their eyes met again. The green of hers was flecked with gold. Ryan looked away, patted the book. She started again toward the door.

"How can I get this back to you?" he said, following her as she weaved through the racks.

"You can have it," she said without turning.

"You're just giving me your book?" A hanger jabbed him in the ribs.

"That's what they're for," she said. She stopped at the entry and looked at him. "Books are meant to be shared."

"At least give me your email," he said. "So I can tell you what I thought." He waved the book at her.

Shay half smiled, like she knew what was really going on here. "You can come with me," she said. "If you're done skirt shopping."

Ryan felt everything in his body relax. *I can go with her.* "I think I have enough skirts at home."

Ryan felt like a criminal stepping over the threshold into the abandoned corridor—the guards must have moved on. Shay simply walked out onto the carpeted hallway and turned toward the escalators. Her strange shirt twirled behind her like a pennant.

"You coming?" she asked, placing a foot onto the stairs. And she was lifted up.

Thad would have told him to just wait, what was the big deal, the last thing Ryan needed was to have a police altercation that might make it back to Coach. Ryan ignored his inner-Thad; he stumbled forward the last few steps and hopped onto the escalator behind her.

Shay explained to him why Tagore was so special. It was her nani who had introduced her to the poet when she was ten, after her grandfather had died. Shay had been miserably sad because her grandfather had been her favorite. Nani said Tagore had been his guide.

"His poems are so lyrical and wise," Shay said. "They speak to my soul."

The last time Ryan had heard someone discuss his soul was in church. He'd never heard anyone sound this juiced about poetry. And no girl, not even his girlfriend, had ever opened up to him like this. He felt drunk. He wanted to tell her things.

He was way out of his comfort zone.

Aéropostale wasn't far from the escalators. Ryan waited by the entry, where he was scowled at by the clerk while Shay circled the store. He was beginning to wonder what Toxic demon had possessed him; the Ryan he knew would not engage in criminal wandering with a girl who talked about her lyrical soul.

Shay appeared at his side. "They must have left." She pulled out an old-school flip-open phone. "Dead, dead, deadski," she said, flipping it closed. "Can I borrow yours?"

Ryan pulled out his Droid and handed it to her.

"Whoa," she said, fake-frowning. "*Fan*-cy." She turned the phone over. "Where are the buttons?"

Ryan slid his finger across the LOCK button.

Shay watched, eyes wide. "We really live in a magical age." She took the phone from him and dialed.

Ryan had never spoken to anyone who said things like "magical age." Or who didn't know how to use a touch-screen. This girl was from another planet, another galaxy. He wondered what she would say next.

"Nani's not answering," Shay said, handing him back the phone. "They might be waiting for me at the car." She took a step, then turned back and hugged Ryan. "Thank you for being so gentlemanly."

He didn't breathe for fear that it might make her let go.

But she did and began power-walking for the exit.

Ryan raced to catch up with her. "What kind of gentle-man doesn't walk a girl to the door?"

Shay held out her arm. "My carriage awaits," she said in a playful, British accent.

Ryan slid his arm into hers. "Onward."

What kind of idiot had he become that he was saying things like *onward*?

The closest mall exit was down a floor, at the end of a short hallway, and consisted of two sets of glass double doors. In the vestibule, two big cops—actual cops with guns in their belts—leaned against a vending machine. Shay didn't so much as blink: She just pushed the first set of doors open and walked in.

The nearer cop blocked her path. "You were told to wait in your store," he said.

Shay looked him in the eyes, her jaw set. "I have to find my grandmother."

Through the glass, Ryan saw that a wall of fencing was being set up around the edge of the mall parking lot. *What the hell kind of security situation is this?*

"You'll have to wait like the rest of the people." The cop crossed his arms. "We going to have a problem?" He looked at Ryan.

"No problem," Ryan replied quickly.

Shay looked at him, tilting her head and pursing her lips. Ryan shrugged. What was he supposed to do, kick the cop's butt?

Shay turned back to the cop. "They said the security problem's in the parking garage," she said. "I just want to go out to the open air lot."

The second cop shuffled over. "I'm going to ask you one more time to go back to your store."

Ryan's phone rang. He pulled it out—a strange number. He tapped Shay on the shoulder. "Maybe this is your grandmother?"

Shay instantly withdrew from her standoff with the cops and took the phone. "Nani?" she said, then began speaking in Indian.

The first cop got on his walkie-talkie. "Security, we have two civilians in the hall at exit one."

The second cop jutted his chin at Ryan. "I've seen you play ball," he said.

Ryan froze. *What if this guy knows Coach?*

"You Jimmy Murphy's kid?"

He knew Dad—*even worse.*

"I'm really sorry," Ryan began. "I mean, she was just really upset and I was trying to help."

The cop clapped him on the shoulder. "Girls, kid," he said. "Don't let them get in the way of what's important." He pushed Ryan through the glass door and let it close between them. He stared hard into Ryan's eyes.

Ryan stepped back and stumbled into Shay.

"They're still here!" she said. "Preeti got hungry, so they went to the food court." She pushed the phone into his chest and began to jog back down the hall.

The cop pointed vigorously at the entrance to the nearest store: PaperClips.

Ryan jammed his hands into his pockets and shuffled into PaperClips.

Shay didn't follow.

S
H
A
Y

Shaila Dixit drove a French fry through the puddle of ketchup on the crumpled wrapper in front of her. It'd been hours since she'd left Ryan in the corridor, but she couldn't stop replaying every second of their half hour together in her mind. The whole day had felt blessed—and then he'd abandoned her.

She'd come to the mall to get out of the house. The place was still a cluttered mess from the move. Shay couldn't sit for five minutes anywhere without being asked to unpack something or *get out of the way, I'm vacuuming!* She was losing her mind.

As if moving itself weren't enough of a nightmare. All her friends had been like, Edison's only an hour away, we'll come visit all the time, but none had come in the four months she'd lived here. More than that, though, instead of Shay the Actress or Shay the Poet—in Stonecliff, she was Shay the Indian Chick.

Shay tried to put on a brave face about it all. During lunch at school, she joked about Mom overdoing it with the cumin. She fashioned outfits out of her Indian garb to better look the part. But her weekends were still an endless expanse of time with no one but Preeti and Nani to fill it. So when she needed to escape, she came to the mall like every other teenager in America. Here, she was normal. Anyone who saw her would think friends were coming to meet her later, maybe they were waiting in another store and she only had to finish this purchase before joining them. When she could no longer pretend, she excused herself and went somewhere to hide in music and poetry. Toxic had seemed as good a place as any.

But then this gorgeous guy had pulled her out of her loneliness. For thirty whole minutes, she'd had a friend. She'd felt ready to explode out of her skin with happiness. But she'd pushed it too far. How could she have expected him to keep following her? Especially when she was basically asking him to disobey the cops. She couldn't have expected it. But she'd hoped.

"Shaila-bhen, when can we go home?" Preeti whined, slumping into the seat next to Shay. They'd been stuck in the food court for hours, staring out the wall of windows at the parking lot as the sun set.

"When they tell us," Shay answered, shoving a fry into her mouth.

Why had she given him her book? He who turned out to be less knight in shining armor than coward with good hair. He'd seemed so enthralled by her—yet another instance of her radar being way off. Ever since the move, Shay felt like she'd been stumbling in the dark. Maybe if her friends had visited like they'd promised, it would be easier to fake the smiles. Maybe if the theater program at her new school didn't suck. Maybe, what if, whatever.

Nani flipped open her phone, then slapped it shut again and shook her head. Their parents had called Nani's phone every fifteen minutes. It was funny to watch her grandmother's surprise and confusion each time the phone rang, like she hadn't noticed the thing existed, even though it was clenched in her fist.

"Perhaps it is for the best," said Nani in Gujarati. "Perhaps by the time we leave, that henna will have worn off and your father won't kill us both." She smiled and shifted on the metal chair.

Shay touched her cheek. She'd snuck into Nani's room the night before and taken the henna, then worked for hours with a flashlight and a hand mirror to create the design. Shay had been in charge of the makeup for all the shows at her old school, meaning the tattoo was awesome, if forbidden. Nani had gasped at seeing her in the morning, then been more than happy when Shay suggested they go to the mall to keep Ba and Bapuji from seeing what Shay had done. Nani could always be counted on to act as a coconspirator.

"We should find you somewhere more comfortable to sit, Nani," Shay said.

Nani patted Shay's hand. "I'm fine."

How would she explain the missing book to Nani? *Oh, I met a cute guy and wanted him to hang around and thought he got that, but then he ditched me and now it's lost, your gift, gone.* Shay felt like a moron.

Preeti, who in all her ten years of life had never been

more annoying, kicked Shay's chair. "I want to go home."

Shay pulled some money from her pocket. "Here," she said. "Go ride the Ferris wheel again."

Preeti snatched up the money and raced for the Ferris wheel. Shay guessed that if they had to be trapped in the mall, they were in the best location. Not only was the food court a huge space with trees and plants, glass walls and ceiling (mostly open, as the third floor slimmed down to a narrow bridge of corridor above them), but opposite the food vendors was a Ferris wheel and merry-go-round. Not much entertainment for Shay, but perfect for keeping Preeti and every other child occupied. The Ferris wheel and merry-go-round were in constant operation.

Those guys must be raking it in, Shay thought. *They should cause a security situation on a regular basis.*

The phone rang: Her parents. Nani spoke with them, her voice rising to match the ascending tones on the other end of the line. Suddenly, Nani shoved the phone at Shay. "They want to talk to you."

Shay took the phone. Her parents immediately started asking the same questions they'd been asking all afternoon. Shay gave them the same answers: "No, they haven't said anything more. No, we can't leave. I already tried. We can't leave the food court. No, I haven't seen any terrorists. Yes, Preeti is fine. I'm sure they'll let us go soon."

Her mother interrupted her father—they were on two different phones, talking over each other. "Nani's medicine. Has she taken her medicine?"

"I don't know," Shay said. She put her hand over the mouthpiece. "Nani? Have you taken your medicine?" *That's right.* Nani had diabetes and needed insulin shots.

Her grandmother looked into her bag. "Yes, tell my daughter. No need to worry."

Shay didn't like the way Nani sounded: She was no longer annoyed. But why make her mother worry? There was nothing her parents could do for Nani on the outside.

Shay took her hand from the phone. "Nani's fine, Ba. We'll call when we hear anything."

She hung up and turned to Nani. "You haven't taken your medication, have you?"

Nani smiled. "No, my dear. I only take it before breakfast and dinner. Who could have known we would be here so late?"

"Do you need insulin?" Shay could not trust Nani's smile. Her grandmother would rather starve than trouble anyone to pass her food at the dinner table.

Upon closer examination, Nani's skin seemed slack and her breathing shallow.

"I'm going to go to the PhreshPharm," Shay said. "It's just down the hall."

"The man told us to wait here," Nani said, but there was no force to her words.

"You need your insulin." Shay squeezed her grandmother's hand. "Watch for Preeti and don't tell her where I went. She'll only try to follow."

Shay didn't run; she walked calmly toward one of the food vendors, as if coming to make a purchase, then banked around the narrow wall of the FrankenHut and into the hallway.

There weren't as many people down at this far end of the mall, or maybe they'd snuck across the hall to the department store—Harry's had a home section full of pillows and beds. Shay considered sneaking Nani down the hall to Harry's but gave up the plan when two mall guards stepped off the escalator. No way Nani could move fast enough to avoid getting caught. Shay ducked behind a plant as the guards passed, then booked it for the pharmacy.

Shay shuffled past the few people splayed on the floor between the rows of toothpaste and deodorant to the back, where the pharmacist was asleep on the counter.

"Excuse me," Shay said, tapping the woman's arm.

The woman woke with a snort. "What, kid?" She stretched and scratched her hair.

"My grandmother needs insulin." Shay laid a twenty onto the counter. "Will this cover it?"

The woman smirked. "You got a prescription?"

"Please," Shay said. "Can you just give me a little? We've been stuck here forever and my grandmother didn't bring any."

The woman sighed. "Look, truth is you're not the first to come here looking for drugs. But we don't stock that much. We ran out of insulin earlier this evening."

Shay was stunned. "Can't you call someone?"

The woman's face loosened into a kind expression. "Honey, if I could call someone, I would be on the phone."

Shay dragged her feet out of the store. They ran out of insulin? What were people supposed to do? She needed to talk to the person in charge. And where would this person be? *The parking garage.*

Someone had turned the escalators and elevators off at this point, so Shay skipped quickly down the stalled steps to the first floor and then ran toward the central courtyard and fountain. It was eerie being the only person in the hallway, seeing the other people trapped behind the glass storefronts like fish in a tank. Some looked up at her as she passed; most did not.

Shay reached the escalators to the garage and steeled herself for a confrontation. She took the steps two at a time, psyching herself up to battle her way to the head honcho. But there was no one to confront. The garage was empty. Shay pushed her way out of the glass-enclosed escalator lobby. She heard voices off to her left.

Two police cruisers were parked in front of a cinder-block room near the Dumpsters, their lights beating red and blue pulses across the dark walls. A kid who looked about her age sat in the backseat of one of the cruisers, his head against the glass. A tired-looking woman sat on the back bumper of the car. A tubby guy in a beige suit stood in front of her waving a piece of paper.

"I've got tenant complaints piling up," he snapped.

"Yours is the least of my problems," the woman said.

Shay had expected a mob of police, tons of lights, cages filled with criminals. This looked like a vandalism case at best.

The woman held up a hand and the tubby man controlled his hysteria. The woman began speaking to no one—then Shay noticed the cell phone earpiece. "How was I supposed to know that regulations required evacuation, not quarantine? With the anthrax scare, the danger was not treating people in time, so I figured you'd want to keep everyone together."

Did she just say quarantine?

"Tell them I knew we should evacuate," the tubby man said. "Make sure they know—"

The woman glared at the guy, who shut up, and continued. "They won't let me evacuate everyone now? Well, it's not like I wanted to increase exposure rates. My goddamned family is trapped here! Fine, tell the Feds that I'm sorry for screwing with their procedure." She dug the ear piece from her ear and slammed it down on the trunk.

This was obviously more than a vandalism case.

"Excuse me?" said Shay, her voice echoing throughout the garage.

The woman looked up. "Oh, god," she said.

The tubby guy stepped forward. "Miss, please return to your store."

"Did you just say we're being quarantined?" Shay stood straighter, preparing herself for that confrontation she'd been waiting for.

A policeman appeared behind her and placed his hands on her shoulders. Shay wrenched her head around. It was the same guy who'd been in the exit doorway.

"This one's been a problem all day, Senator." The cop pushed Shay toward the squad car. "Tried to bust out the exit."

The woman—the senator—looked at her watch, then buttoned her blazer. "I'd better make the announcement."

"What announcement?" Shay shouted, struggling in the policeman's grasp. "Can we go home?"

The senator straightened her collar. "We're not going home for a while."

"But my grandmother needs her medicine!" Shay could

not believe how calm this woman was. "You have to take care of her!"

The senator looked at the policeman. "Put her in with the other kid until I get back." The tubby man followed the senator into the shadows.

"I have to get back to my grandmother!" Shay shouted as the cop dragged her to the car.

The policeman shoved her into the cruiser without another word and slammed the door.

The boy looked at Shay. "What'd they get you for?" he asked, smiling like this was all some big joke.

"I have to get out of this car," Shay said, jimmying the door handle.

"You're not getting out that way," he said.

"What did you do to lock down the mall? Call in a bomb threat?"

"No threat," he said calmly. "I found a bomb. They're not sure yet whether to believe me when I said I didn't put it there. I've been stuck here since this morning."

Shay stopped jiggling the door handle. "Are you serious?"

The speakers squealed to life. The senator's voice boomed around the garage. "Excuse me, I have an announcement. The security situation is ongoing, and as such you are asked to remain in your stores for the time being. You have been extremely patient, and in appreciation for your patience, you will each be given a twenty-five-dollar gift certificate for use anywhere in the mall. We'll be coming around to take your names and make sure you get your certificate. In addition, pizza will be served in all the stores.

"We are aware that some people are in need of services. We ask that each store identify a spokesperson, and that that person create a list of all the individuals in their store as well as any urgent needs such as medical or hygienic requirements that must be addressed. Supplies will be delivered to each store according to the lists of individuals created by the spokesperson.

"A security guard will be visiting each store to bring its residents to the bathroom facilities. If the store you are in has facilities available to it, please use those and not the general ones in the corridors.

"We continue to assess the security situation and hope to have further updates in the near future. I thank you, again, for your patience."

The speaker squealed and went dead.

"Guess we'll be here for a while," the guy said. "Best we get acquainted. I'm Marco." He held out a hand.

Shay glanced at him, ignored his hand. "Shay." She returned her attention to the door.

"Don't worry about the bomb," he said, a sarcastic lilt to his voice. "The cops sent in a robot to test it for radioactivity. Early reports show it's not a nuke."

"How comforting," Shay managed.

The woman returned. On her signal, the policeman let both Shay and Marco out of the cruiser. "Go back to your grandmother," she said to Shay. "And Marco, you go back up to the Grill'n'Shake. We've got a long night ahead of us."

"What about my grandmother's medicine?" Shay asked. "She needs insulin."

The woman walked past them to her phone on the car's

trunk. "I'll add it to the list." She dialed the phone and disappeared into a conversation.

The policeman patted Shay on the shoulder. "I'll walk you to your grandmother," he said. He pushed her forward, toward the elevators. It wasn't a request.

On the first floor, as they passed the main entrance, Shay noticed that the windowed doors were now blocked by concrete barriers and that sandbags were being laid against the glass.

The cop caught her staring. "Welcome to your new home, kid."   ✦

DAY

TWO

· SUNDAY ·

L
E
X
I

exi lay motionless under the table. If she didn't
move, maybe it wouldn't be morning. It would still
be last night.

How weird to think that the best night of her life would
be when she was trapped in the CommerceDome with a
bunch of strangers. Then again, Ginger wasn't a stranger
anymore. Last night, Lexi felt the same connection with
her that she had gaming with Darren. It was like they
were one brain moving the avatars on the screen, as
they worked on turning their clip into a short film. For
hours. They didn't even notice how long they'd been
working until Dad brought over two slices of pizza.

When the announcement was made that they were all
being held overnight, of course Ginger called her mom,
but she got right off and was like, "What's next?" and began sliding through the keyframes they'd already finished.

Later, once it was dark and everyone else was asleep,

Lexi offered to show Ginger her own movie—not even Darren had seen her movie. As it played, Lexi watched Ginger. Once it was over, Ginger said it was as good as any Pixar film, and Lexi knew from her reactions while it'd played that she meant it.

"Hey, you up?"

Ginger knelt beside Lexi's camp under the computer. Ginger had slept across the aisle under the iPad display. The night before, two security guards had come around with blankets and pillows pilfered from the various home stores in the mall. Lexi ended up with a rainbow-colored comforter coated with unicorns, and Ginger's was a weird green color with an old-lady flower pattern.

"I barely slept, I was so uncomfortable," Ginger continued. "When the lights came on, I was sort of still in a dream—has that ever happened to you?—and I had completely forgotten where I was, so I sat straight up and whacked my head into the table." She rubbed her forehead for emphasis.

Lexi shuffled into a sit. Her brain began scratching together an appropriate response. Talking was so different from texting—one had to string words together so quickly in real life. Maybe she should suggest breakfast? She glanced around to see where her dad was. Maybe they could go to the Pancake Palace?

"There's going to be a run on the bathrooms," Ginger said, rummaging under her comforter. She pulled out her purse and began picking through its contents. She extracted a small packet of breath-freshening wafers and slipped one into her mouth. She turned to Lexi. "Want one?"

"Thanks," Lexi muttered. She nearly gagged on the explosion of mint.

Ginger pulled out her phone and began flicking through her texts. Should Lexi get out her phone too? Should they compare texts?

As if rescuing her from her own brain, the Senator's voice boomed over the mall loudspeaker: "Patrons of the Shops at Stonecliff, I regret to inform you that the security situation remains ongoing. Federal officials have been brought in to assist in the investigation. Given the nature of the investigation, we cannot allow any individual to leave the mall at this time. You may, however, leave the stores and move freely around the mall. The parking level remains closed. If you require access to the parking level, please consult with a customer service representative at the first-floor kiosk opposite the Borderlands Cantina. Please do not attempt to exit the mall. We are working to resolve this situation as quickly as possible."

Ginger sucked in her breath. "Oh my god, Maddie totally kissed a senior last night!" She pushed Lexi's shoulder like Lexi should be shocked. At school, Maddie always seemed to be hanging off some boy. It was no surprise to Lexi that Maddie had locked lips with one while unsupervised for an entire night.

"You want to get a bagel?" Lexi said.

Ginger was furiously texting, fingers flying over the little keys. "Huh?" she said. "Bagel?" She finished typing, then looked up. "I'd love to," she said, "but Maddie wants me to meet these guys at Abercrombie." She dug a tiny tub of sparkly pink lip gloss out of her bag and slid some across her lips with her pinky, then stood and straightened her sweater over her jeans. Ginger had the perfect body—no gargantuan boobs or butt ballooned off her lithe ballerina frame. She ran her fingers through her hair, flipping her head first one way, then the other as she glowered at her reflection in the store's glass wall.

"All right," she said, finally standing still. She locked eyes with Lexi. "Do I look okay? Like okay enough to meet a senior?" Her eyebrows were arched in a hopeful expression.

Part of Lexi wanted to slap Ginger—the girl who'd thrilled at morphing a cloud across a CG sky had been completely subsumed by this boy-obsessed bubblehead. But the other part won control. "You look great," she said.

Apparently, Lexi had provided the correct response: Ginger stooped to give her a quick hug. "I had such a great time last night!" she said, and began walking to the door.

"I'll see you later?" Lexi asked. But Ginger was already in the hallway. She didn't look back.

Lexi sank down onto her comforter. Of course Ginger left the instant she could. What else had Lexi expected? Their friendship had been a one-night-only event, a product of circumstance.

Lexi hunted around in her messenger bag for her phone. Its battery was low; it had been buzzing all night with texts. All from Darren. She opened the first message: *You still at CommerceDome? On news.* The second: *Mall lockdown? What's happening?* The next twenty were all in the same vein. *Is it the zombie apocalypse? Anyone resorting to cannibalism?*

Strangely, Darren's texts made her feel worse. Not one of them expressed interest in whether she herself was okay. These could have been texts sent to anyone. And for a moment, a vast emptiness opened inside Lexi, a sucking need so strong she felt she might disappear inside it.

No. She would not fall apart in this rainbow-unicorn cave. Darren was just being his funny self. If he weren't worried, he wouldn't have texted in the first place.

She tried to call him and got an all-circuits-are-busy message. So she sent a text that could go through as soon as some bandwidth opened up. *Still here, trapped. But had full access to computer and new BXE Fillion card so was all gud. Will find out whazzup.*

Lexi heard tromping footsteps and turned to see the Senator barrel in from the hall. The sight of her converted all Lexi's sadness to rage. This entire situation was the Senator's fault.

Dad stood, his head and shoulders rising above the shelf he'd been hidden behind, and hugged the Senator. She practically fell into his arms. She looked bad, wiped out. And not from the usual committee politics.

"If I kill the mall manager," Dotty said, "will you support my insanity defense?"

"The man's a troll," Arthur said. "No one would even question you."

For a moment, Lexi felt some sympathy for her mother. But then she recalled her mission—Darren (her real friend; her only friend) needed to know what was going on. Lexi could stand talking to her mother to help Darren.

Dad caught Lexi staring and waved her over. "Maybe now we can finally catch some of that quality family time?" he said. "Anyone as hungry for pancakes as I am?"

He smiled at the Senator, who reached a hand out to

wipe something from Lexi's cheek. Lexi flinched away from her touch.

"I'm afraid I'll have to pass," the Senator said, frowning. "But you guys have fun."

Dad grimaced. "You have to eat," he said.

"I will," the Senator answered.

Lexi had never known the Senator to miss breakfast. The woman was a breakfast nut—"Most important meal of the day!" was a favorite tagline.

"What's going on in the parking garage?" Lexi asked. "And don't say nothing because I have never heard you neg a pancake invitation before."

The Senator dropped her hand onto Lexi's shoulder. "Nothing you need to worry about," she said. "Have fun at breakfast." She kissed Lexi's head and made for the door.

"HAVE FUN"??? A kiss on the head? I'm not a freaking child!

Dad watched the Senator as she wove her way into the herd in the hall. "Guess it's just you and me, kiddo."

Lexi glared at her mother—the Senator was lying through her perfectly whitened teeth. She had to find out what was really going on.

"Sorry, but Ginger asked me to meet her at Abercrombie," she said, her tongue tripping over the lie.

Her dad's eyes lit up. "The girl from Irvington? From last night?"

Arthur was way too excited. Like it was so unusual for Lexi to meet a friend somewhere. Like Ginger was so great.

"Have fun," he said, too quickly. "If you need me, I'll be in line at the Pancake Palace along with the rest of the

mall." He waved at the crowd forming in front of the restaurant down the hall.

Lexi exited the store and followed where the Senator had
gone. It didn't take long to locate her. She moved with
purpose while everyone else in the crowd rambled aimlessly across the carpet. Lexi guessed her mother was the
only person who had anywhere to be.

There were huge lines outside all of the restaurants,
each monitored by a security guard. If the security situation was so serious, where were the real police? Why
leave crowd control to the hack mall brigade?

The Senator turned down a corridor toward the exits.
Lexi hid behind a mall directory and watched where her
mother went. Temporary walls had been erected around a
store near the end of the hall, blocking it from view. Lexi
checked the map and saw that it was a PaperClips. Or had
been a PaperClips. She dashed down the hallway.

There were few people in this area of the mall. Between the blocked exits and walled-off PaperClips, there
was little else down this corridor but a Domestic Decor,
and the only people in there were a couple of boys shoot-
ing zombies on the Xbox display. Lexi had beaten every
level of that game—she could have pwned them right and
proper. But she had other things on her mind.

There were no guards at the flimsy wall erected around
the PaperClips. It was made from sheets of thin press-
board, the stuff Lexi had seen kids make ramps out of
for their bikes, covered in white paper with the words
"Guess what's coming to Stonecliff?" printed in a styl-
ish blue font. A door had been cut into the boards, and

Lexi peered through the doorknob hole drilled into it.

The PaperClips entrance was covered over with sheets of clear plastic. When the sheets flapped, she could see her mother near the cash registers. She was talking to a short guy in a bad suit—*the mall manager?* Other people in uniforms (mall security and what had to be maintenance guys) moved crates of paper and boxes of pens away from the center of the room. Why were they messing with the PaperClips? *I thought the security problem was in the garage . . .*

Lexi pulled on the door hole. To her surprise, the door opened—there was no lock. Her mother was trying to make this overnight transformation look as inconspicuous as possible. *Nothing to see here, folks! Just a complete redesign of a PaperClips in the middle of a mall crisis. Not strange at all.*

Lexi slipped through the door and pulled it closed behind her. No one seemed to notice. She crept to the store entrance. When the plastic flapped, she ducked inside and hid behind a display of markers and crayons.

"So they're sure it's not a dirty bomb, but that's about it?" the mall manager asked.

Lexi's heart skipped a beat. *Did he just say* BOMB*?!?!?!?!* She held her breath so she wouldn't miss a word.

"That's what they're telling me," the Senator said. Her phone rang; she answered, then whispered to the manager, "They're here."

The manager followed her to the back wall of the store and through the stockroom doors.

Lexi could not get to the stockroom doors without being seen. The guards were still clearing the main floor, pushing the displays against the permanent shelving along the interior walls. She'd have to make a run for it across the open floor.

But then the doors opened and a person in a space suit—not space suit, but some creepy blue plastic hazmat suit with a giant enclosed hood—pushed a cart loaded with machines and boxes into the room. Behind him, Lexi saw that the loading dock's door had been covered over with overlapping thick plastic strips, and beyond that was a giant tunnel of plastic. Several more hazmat-suited people walked up the tunnel and pushed through the plastic with other carts piled with machines and boxes.

Lexi ducked back behind her display. This was like some bad science fiction movie. Or the opening of that video game where you knew you were facing the zombie apocalypse when the evil government scientists showed up to quarantine the city.

"We'll place the triage area over here," a muffled voice said. *Must be the hazmat person.* Lexi froze. The voice sounded far too close for her comfort. "We'll need another wall across there to hide the observation and diagnostic units."

"The PaperClips representative said their insurance required someone at FEMA to sign off on all the paperwork." *Nasal whine—has to be the mall troll.*

"I think we should curtain the windows." Lexi recognized her mother's voice. "To keep the people from panicking."

The muffled voice laughed—at least, Lexi thought it

laughed. "If you think curtains will help, we'll bring them in."

This was worse than the zombie apocalypse. This was actually happening.

Lexi bolted out of the PaperClips the second she had the chance. The Senator wasn't overreacting. She wasn't just trying to avoid her daughter. This was not all the Senator's fault.

She ran down the hall, not stopping until she hit the main corridor. She rested a hand on the edge of the central fountain. Strangers crowded around her. A thousand voices echoed through the cavernous space. A woman lugging a bag fat with purchases shoved Lexi's hips, nearly knocking her into the rippling water. Her head began to spin. Too many people. Too loud.

Her feet steered her up the escalator toward Abercrombie & Fitch. There were a bunch of high school kids there. Crowds of them hovered near the entrance, whispering and texting and laughing.

Ginger appeared. Not Lexi's Ginger, but the other Ginger. Maddie's Ginger. She was laughing little yips like a neurotic terrier. Maddie had her fingers wrapped around the thick arm of a giant dude in a football jersey. Another jerseyed hunk hovered behind Ginger, eyes peeling the layers of clothing from her body.

They did not look like they were interested in discussing dirty bombs and triage units. These were not her people.

Before Lexi could turn tail, Ginger spotted her and waved hysterically, like she was actually happy to see her.

When Lexi failed to move closer, Ginger trotted toward her. The hunk followed.

"How many sexy friends does Maddie have?" he said, lips curling into a snarl. "That ass looks good enough to eat."

It took Lexi a second to realize that the ass to which he was referring was her own.

Ginger smacked the guy on the arm and giggled. "Mi-*ike*," she cooed.

Lexi had no idea how to respond to this guy. The lupine look on his face made her want to vomit. And why was Ginger hanging on him? The floor tilted. She needed to sit down.

"I'm looking for my dad," she said. "I'll see you later."

"Okay," Ginger said, tugging her boy in Maddie's direction.

"Later," the guy said, voice dripping with slime.

Lexi unlocked her phone and tried Darren again. All circuits were still busy. She had to find a landline. But there was a crowd by the pay phones at the exit. Probably all the public phones were mobbed.

Then it came to her: There was another way—*Wi-Fi*. Lexi ran back to the Apple Store. Glancing around to make sure no one was looking, she picked up an iPad. (If only she hadn't lost her iPhone, a crime for which the Senator had sentenced her to wireless purgatory on a cheap iKnockoff.) She turned off its security settings, opened the app store, and searched for WebPhone. She typed that yes, she wanted to try WebPhone for free, confirmed that she was over eighteen, got a login under her father's name, and downloaded the program.

When the icon appeared on the screen, she opened the program and dialed in Darren's home phone number. His mom picked up. Lexi guessed that she didn't know about her being trapped in the mall, because she simply screamed to Darren that he had a call.

"Lexi?" Darren said when he got on the line.

"Like anyone else knows your number," Lexi said. A flood of relief poured through her body talking to him. She felt like crying.

"What is going on over there?" he said. Lexi could hear him shuffling back to his room. "Every news station keeps showing the same stock footage of the mall. There's no live coverage."

"I don't know," Lexi said. "Some people in hazmat suits said something about triage."

"Some people in *what*?" Darren yelped.

"Hey!" a saleswoman yelled from the back of the store. "Put that tablet down! There's no public Internet use!" She began to make her way toward Lexi.

"I'll call back later," she said to Darren, then tapped the icon, ending the call, and trashed the program, deleting it from the tablet.

The woman reached her. "I saw you talking. You downloaded a program."

"No, I didn't," Lexi said calmly, casually, like lying and hacking were part of her daily routine. She walked out of the store as if she hadn't a care in the world, then, upon reaching a bench, crumpled onto the seat.

Alone again. A hacker, a criminal. A bad daughter. And threatened by something in this mall that required the employment of hazmat suits.

A hand dropped onto her shoulder.

"Couldn't find Ginger?" Her dad sat beside her.

Tears amassed along the borders of Lexi's eyes. She looked at her father's blithe, smiling face.

"Do you know what Mom's doing in the PaperClips?"

Her father swore under his breath; this from the man who yelled at her for taking the Lord's name in vain.

"If you saw that place, you know how serious this situation is," he said.

She had no idea about anything, but it felt good to lean against her dad. Even if he clearly didn't plan to tell her anything about what was really going on.

"Are we gonna be okay?" she asked him.

"Your mom is taking care of things."

And this is supposed to be a comfort?

He hugged her to him. "You want to get something to eat?" he asked. Dad was a big believer in the healing power of food, as one could tell from the slight paunch hanging over his belt.

"I could really use some pancakes," Lexi admitted.

"I know just the place," he said.

They stood, two Rosses against the insane horror show that the CommerceDome had become, and strolled toward the massive line streaming into the Pancake Palace.

RYAN

It took Ryan an hour and a half to get through the line to go to the bathroom. By the time he reached the stall, he had composed his apology to Shay for being such a coward yesterday afternoon. All night, he had replayed their good-bye through his mind, run through various heroic scenarios in which he tackled the one cop while toppling the vending machine onto the other cop, creating an opening for her to bust out of the mall. Or he took her hand and dashed with her up the escalator and she kissed him and said he was awesome. Anything but him pretending she didn't exist and shuffling, head down, into the PaperClips.

While constructing these scenarios, he flipped through the book Shay had given him—normally, if he read anything, he read magazines, and then mostly just the tags under the pictures, but last night was far from normal. Shay's book was full of weird, long poems, a bunch of them love poems. Some of the love stuff was kind of, well, how else could he put it, sexy. He kept looking over his shoulder at the other people camped out in the Paper-Clips like he was afraid of being caught reading it, like old-timey poetry from India was the equivalent of one of Thad's porno mags. But he couldn't put it down.

In reading it, he felt like he was seeing a part of Shay that maybe he shouldn't. He didn't know her well enough to know that she had also read these poems. He wondered if she found them sexy. He wondered if she knew what Tagore was talking about when he said, "I offered you my youth's foaming wine," and did it mean what Ryan thought it meant?

Ryan needed to know the answers to these questions. He had to find Shay. And the first thing he needed to do when he found her was apologize for being such a loser. This Tagore guy would never have left her standing in the hallway to fend for herself. The man who had the guts to write to some girl, "I seem to have loved you in number-less forms, numberless times, in life after life, in age after age, forever" (Like you'd ever tell a girl something like that! Like she wouldn't laugh in your face!) was not a man who'd have run away from a couple of mall cops.

Ryan decided he would check out the food court first. That was where Shay had been headed and she might not have left yet.

It was close to ten in the morning and the mall seemed strangely calm. The people who weren't waiting to get into one of the restaurants were window-shopping or actually going into the stores to buy stuff, maybe with their gift certificates. Families were camped out in the open spaces on the first floor, and children screamed and laughed and chased each other around the benches. Ryan could almost pretend that there wasn't some vague security situation holding them all hostage.

Figuring he should check in with his mom to let her know he'd survived the night, Ryan felt around for his phone and realized he'd left it in his jacket—which he'd left in the PaperClips. He bolted back down the corridor, turned the corner, and saw that the PaperClips was gone. It was now a plywood wall. *What the hell?* He'd only been gone an hour and a half.

He walked up to the wall and found that there was a door cut into it with a small hole for a doorknob. Ryan peered through the hole. The whole place was covered with plastic tarps and blue curtains. And then a woman in a hazmat suit stepped through the swinging doors from the stockroom.

"We're going to need air samples from the affected areas." The woman's voice was raspy like a machine's.

Ryan stumbled backward and landed on his butt. Why was a lady in a hazmat suit in the PaperClips? His heart raced, the ceiling pressed down—he had to get away. He loped down the hall, forgetting about his jacket, his phone, desperate to find Shay.

"Whoa!" shouted a familiar voice. "Where you running to, Jumbo Shrimp?"

The walls retreated; his pulse slowed. Ryan turned and saw two guys from the team, Mike Richter and Drew Bonner, strolling down the main hall toward him. They'd dubbed him Jumbo Shrimp when he was a frosh for being bigger than half the JV team and younger than most of them by a year. It wasn't the greatest nickname, but Ryan was just happy to get one. Thad said that not every guy did.

Ryan held out his hand for a shoulder bump, which was how these guys said hello. "Where'd you guys get stuck last night?" he asked. He was a regular guy on the football team, not some freaked-out kid who just saw something out of a sci-fi nightmare.

Richter punched Bonner's arm. "Bright Light here wanted to check out the chicks in Abercrombie and so we had to sleep on a pile of winter coats."

"With a bunch of hot chicks." Bonner mimed smacking an ass and humping it. He snatched the book from Ryan's back pocket. "What fine reading material do we have here?"

Ryan's pulse sped up a notch. These were not the kind of guys you discussed your lyrical soul with. "Just something I found in PaperClips," he said, covering. "I got stuck sleeping on a stack of printer paper."

Drew flipped through the pages. "Dude, this book looks lame." He shoved it back at Ryan. "You might want to upgrade to something that isn't falling apart."

"Right," Ryan said, shoving the book back into his pocket, saying a small prayer.

Mike threw an arm around Ryan's shoulders. "Thad's like a brother to me, J. Shrimp," he said. "He would kill me if I didn't watch your back in this place." Mike ran his fist over Ryan's skull. "So stick with us!"

Ryan ducked out of Mike's attack, laughing. "All right!" he cried. "I'm sure my brother will be grateful."

"You bet your ass he'll be grateful." Mike began walking again; Drew and Ryan followed.

They headed up to the Chop House on the third floor, where they got on line to grab some breakfast. Ryan fingered the two bills in his wallet: a twenty, which was for his zombie makeup, and the gift certificate, which he figured he should save for dinner. But he *was* hungry, and breakfast was the most important meal of the day. Then again, he'd be hungrier later. He kept going back and forth as they snaked through the line. When they finally reached the registers, Ryan didn't order anything.

Mike gave him a stern look. "Lose any weight and I'm downgrading you to plain Shrimp," he said.

"I'm short on cash," Ryan mumbled, hoping he didn't sound as lame as he felt.

Mike shoved one of his burgers at Ryan. "Thad's going to owe me huge, I can tell."

After the three devoured their meals, Mike and Drew leaned against the railing in the corridor.

"There's nothing to *do*," Drew grumbled. He hacked up some phlegm and spat it at the nearest trash can, missing by a foot.

"Gross, dude," Mike said.

Drew burped. "No, *that* was gross," he said. "Burger is so foul coming up."

"We should be at practice," Ryan said, noticing the time. It was now half past ten.

Mike kicked the glass wall. "Coach is going to go ballistic." He stared out at the mall, then swept his hair from his face and squinted his eyes. "You guys feel like a game of touch?"

"Two on Shrimp?" Drew asked, punching Ryan in the shoulder.

"No," Mike said, a snarky smile twisting his lips. "Three on Tarrytown's offensive linemen." He pointed to the first-floor fountain, where there sat four guys from the Tarrytown varsity team. Tarrytown had defeated West Nyack in a squeaker Friday night—part of the reason Ryan had come to the mall was to avoid his brother; Thad was no fun to be around after a loss.

Drew punched his fists on the metal tube of the railing. "Yes!" He lurched down the walkway toward the escalator. "Time for Jumbo Shrimp to man up."

Ryan could not wait to man up with these two.

Drew went to Shep's Sporting Goods and got a football. Mike and the Tarrytown guys scoped out the best location for the game, settling on the first-floor lounge area outside Harry's department store. Ryan tagged along, trying to look useful by carrying Mike's half-empty Sportade bottle.

Drew came back with the ball and the guys started dragging the trash bins into some semblance of a goal post at either end of the lounge. Other kids sensed their plan and asked to join the game. By the time everything was set up, they had two sides of eleven players, and plenty of volunteers should they need more. A crowd developed around the edge of the lounge area's rug.

Mike was running back and Drew a guard, so that left Ryan to take position as quarterback. Normally, he played wide receiver, but he was meant to be QB. In other words, he felt like a freaking god. The Tarrytown guys formed up opposite Drew—they were all linemen, as Mike had said. The stragglers from the crowd took up the other positions. Guys who looked to be from the local community college asked Ryan where to stand and he told them without missing a beat. Mike smiled at him from his position near the planters; Ryan nodded his head in as cool a manner as possible.

A fat guy who claimed to coach a Pop Warner team offered to ref and someone in the crowd scrounged up a whistle. Drew had gotten colored socks from Shep's to use as flags, and each player had a pair tucked into his waist, but from the grim snarls plastered across every guy's face, Ryan was not sure they would be used. It didn't take long for the trash talk to start—emotions were running high. They'd all been trapped in a mall for nearly twenty-four hours and none had had a decent night's sleep. Everyone, even the crowd, was impatient to start the game. Ryan cracked his knuckles.

Ryan had memorized all the plays from the team's book, but in this situation, Mike had simply said, "Throw to me." It seemed as good a plan as any. When the whistle blew, Ryan took the snap from the center, then threw a short pass to Richter. He plowed through some scrawny kid playing linebacker and dashed for the trash-bin goal posts. The Tarrytown guys didn't bother holding their positions; they made straight for Mike. The whole concept of "touch" football did not seem to have registered with them. Ryan guessed they had some unfinished business from Friday's game, given the speed at which they hunted Mike. But Mike was like a freaking cheetah and beat them through the bins. He spiked the ball and everyone screamed like it was the final TD of the Super Bowl.

Ryan played as if his very life depended upon winning this game. Forget that they were in a mall playing touch on a patch of rug barely half the size of a regulation field with a bunch of guys who'd last played football on an Xbox; this was Ryan's first gig as QB and he was not going to blow it. When a Tarrytown guy busted through the line on the snap to sack, Ryan sprang over his shoulders and ran the play in for a touchdown. Mike screamed like some cannibal in from the hunt and hugged Ryan with a ferocity that felt like it left bruises across his back.

Even the crowd got into it, shrieking and hooting with each play. More and more people gathered around them, and crowds formed against the banisters of each of the floors above. The cheers echoed up and down the corridors of the mall. Ryan took a brief moment to take it all in and got smashed by a Tarrytown end.

Drew shoved the guy in the chest. "What the hell, Martin? He hadn't even called the snap." Drew hooked an arm around Ryan and dragged him to his feet. "You cool, J. Shrimp?"

Ryan rubbed his temple. "Yeah," he said. "All good."

"Kid was, like, spaced," the Tarrytown guy said, defending himself from the boos of the onlookers. His teammates gathered around him; together, they formed a menacing huddle.

Mike strutted to Ryan's side and slapped an arm around his shoulders. "I'm sure Thad will appreciate that you flattened his brother, no matter the reason."

"Screw Thad," one of the dudes said.

"You upset that he nailed you on that first down Friday?" Mike asked. "Let me clear it up for you, it wasn't an accident."

The Tarrytown kid lunged at Mike. Ryan threw his

shoulder into the guy's path and nailed him in his solar plexus. The kid fell to his knees, breathless.

The rest of the Tarrytown line stepped forward. One grabbed Ryan's collar.

"Break it up!" A mall cop thrust his way onto the rug-field. He strode up to the group of them. "You boys have caused a bit of a ruckus."

"It's just a game, officer," Mike said. The other guys loosened their fists, like they were all just pals playing a friendly game of pickup.

"We got to set up beds," the officer said. "Clear out."

A few other mall guards began breaking up the audience and the straggler players wandered back to wherever they had come from. The Tarrytown guys flashed Ryan a look like they'd see him later, and Drew smashed a fist into his hand to clarify that the Jumbo Shrimp was spoken for.

Mike jutted his chin at the Tarrytown guys as they disappeared into the masses. "Nice move with the shoulder, J. Shrimp," he said. He smirked at Drew. "Now, I feel like gnawing on a Taco."

"I need to pound something," Drew growled.

Ryan had no idea what they were talking about, but he was not about to leave their side.

Mike led the way up to the top floor. The whole trip, Drew and Mike were doing a play-by-play of the game.

"When you tanked that skinny guy, I thought he was going to puke!" Drew honked a laugh.

"Nothing beats J. Shrimp here hurdling Leon and taking it in for the kill." Mike noogied Ryan's head, then pushed him away with a laugh. It was something Thad would have done.

"Just playing the game, my brothers," Ryan said, cool as anything, though inside he was bouncing like a five-year-old hopped up on sugar.

Mike led the way to the Grill'n'Shake and waited for the hostess. "We'd like a table," he said when she appeared, "in *his* area." Mike pointed at a scrawny kid laboring under a giant tub of dirty dishes.

"Marco?" the girl said. "He's a busboy, not a server. This way." She pinched three menus between her pink-clawed fingers and led them through a maze of tables to a booth in the back of the restaurant.

"We eating?" Ryan asked.

Mike scanned the restaurant. "We can eat," he said, slapping his dad's credit card on the table.

Ryan was fine with just a chicken sandwich and a Coke, but Mike and Drew ordered wings, a fried onion thing, potato skins, and two chicken sandwiches each.

"A growing boy's got to eat," Drew said, winking at the waitress. She rolled her eyes in response.

While they ate, Mike and Drew rambled on to Ryan about their conquests over the years. Ryan knew of Mike and Drew's reputation for preying on the weak, but he'd had no idea how much time they devoted to their efforts. It was like every second they were off the field, they were at work on their latest target. They liked to study a kid, really get under his skin, then tear him apart from the inside.

"Remember when we caught VanEmburgh waxing his chest?"

"I had no idea that stuff would actually rip his skin," Mike said, holding his hands up like, *Whatcha gonna do?*

With each story, Ryan found it harder to muster a laugh. If it weren't for Thad, he might be on the wrong side of Mike and Drew's equation and end up having his head dunked into a toilet for buying the wrong kind of chips.

"That brings us to Taco," Mike said, swinging a thumb in the direction of the skinny busboy. "Dinged my car with his bike."

Drew leaned in to Ryan. "We took care of the bike," he said. "But the kid's still got some pain coming his way."

Taco—the hostess had called him Marco—did not look like he needed any more pain. His apron was wrinkled and dirty, and he looked like he'd been working all day without a break. Ryan knew that he should intervene, save this poor loser from whatever hurt Drew and Mike intended for him. But Ryan's inner devil spoke the truth: Why stick your neck out for some kid you don't even know, especially when it means driving off the only two allies you have in this place? Ryan kept his trap shut.

Mike and Drew loitered in the booth until the table next to them left and needed to be cleared. Marco had avoided their row since they arrived, but now he had no choice but to sling his empty bin over his shoulder and walk as bravely as possible into enemy territory.

"What's up, Taco?" Mike said, turning in his seat and draping his arms over the seat back.

The kid didn't even flinch. "I've got bigger problems than you," he said. He dumped a soda into the bin, then stacked the plates and slid them on top.

"I highly doubt that," Mike said.

The kid snorted—laughed, even. Ryan wondered if perhaps the guy had lost his mind from being overworked.

"Someday soon, Richter," Marco said, "you're going to feel like a real moron for saying that."

Mike nearly hurdled over the seat back. Drew threw himself across the table and grabbed his friend's arm, cocking his head to indicate the approach of an old balding guy.

The old guy—the manager, Ryan guessed—folded his arms across his chest and stood beside Marco. "We have a problem here, boys?" He looked like one of those old guys you messed with at your own risk.

Mike slid back into his seat. "No problem," he said.

"I think it's time for your check," the manager said, sliding a black holder across the tabletop.

As he paid at the hostess station, Mike muttered, "This is so not over."

A sinking feeling took hold of Ryan's gut, which when combined with the greasy chicken, made him feel sick. But sick was weak and weak was crap, so Ryan stowed it and followed Mike and Drew out into the throng.

S
H
A
Y

Shay huddled under the bowed branches of the stunted tree stuck in the giant pot beside Nani's table in the food court, a wrinkled scrap of paper pressed against her jeans. On it was one of her poems. She'd written it Friday, part of an assignment for English due Monday. They were studying haiku, and Shay had drafted several as she sat alone in the courtyard during her free period. The one in her lap had been her favorite:

> *The summer of birds*
> *ends in migration to cliffs,*
> *the fall of dead leaves.*

Shay named the seasons of her life: the winter of the ice trees, the spring of chicken pox and mono. Last summer had been the summer of birds. She'd seen them everywhere, more than normal, always twittering in the shadows. On the day of the move, a flock of crows lurked in the trees around her old house as if hoping to steal the boxes on their way to the truck. She'd tentatively dubbed this season the fall of dead leaves. Given her present situation, stuck under green leaves in the calculated warmth of the glassed-in food court, threatened by a bomb of unknown-but-not-nuclear composition, she felt a new name was in order.

Pulling a pen from her bag, she scratched out *leaves,* but left *dead. Dead* what? *People* had too many syllables.

She crumpled the poem and tossed it into the mulch of the pot. She turned up her iPod and tried to lose herself in the blaring bass line.

Nani was still hunched over her Sudoku. Shay had bought her a thick book of puzzles that morning after the mall cop announced that shoppers were allowed to roam the halls. Last night, a customer service rep had brought Nani some insulin. Nani, however, still did not seem one hundred percent okay. She sighed a lot. Her skin looked ashy. She had bags under her eyes. In the darkest moments—between songs, when someone's shouts echoed around the mall—Shay couldn't help but wonder if it had something to do with the bomb.

Shay hadn't said anything to Nani or Preeti about the bomb. What could she say? "Oh, by the way, there might be a bomb in the basement and we could all be dead by sunrise"? Not the kind of thing to share over a dinner of fried rice and tofu. The only person she could talk to was the boy from the police car—Marco—and he was upstairs at the Grill'n'Shake. Shay was desperate to talk to him, if only to have someone nearby who was as petrified as she, who knew what was really going on. The only problem was how to convince Nani and Preeti to leave the food court—to go to another restaurant.

Shay's contacts were killing her, but she couldn't ditch them entirely; she did not need the world to fall any further out of focus. *Time for another visit to the Phresh-Pharm.* Maybe her old friend at the pharmacy counter could get her solution and a case. She'd been so helpful the first time around.

"I need to get some stuff at the pharmacy," Shay said, turning off her music and sliding down from the pot. "Can I get you anything?"

Nani did not look up from her puzzle. "Take Preeti with you," she said.

"Do you need more medicine, Nani?" Shay asked, kneeling beside her grandmother.

Nani waved a hand at Shay. "Go, my love," she said. "I am fine here with my puzzle." She looked at Shay, pressed her palm to Shay's cheek, then went back to the Sudoku. Even just that quick glance at Nani's face revealed that Nani was anything but fine.

Preeti stood in the line for the Ferris wheel. She was giggling with some other girls who looked about her age. Shay wanted to scream at them. How could they be laughing when there was a freaking bomb in the basement? But they didn't know about the bomb. *Thank god*—Shay could not deal with a shrieking mob of panicked fifth-grade girls.

"We are going for a walk," Shay said, grabbing her sister by the shirtsleeve.

Preeti tugged the fabric from Shay's fist. "No way," she said. "We're going to ride up to the top and then drop popcorn on the boys when they're at the bottom." She pointed to a gang of short, scruffy boys near the front of the line.

"No, you're not," Shay said, grabbing Preeti's arm.

"They did it first!" Preeti cried, wriggling out of Shay's grasp once again.

Shay ran her fingers through her hair. It felt greasy—she must look disgusting. "Fine," she said, sighing for emphasis. "You can ride one more time, then I need to go to the pharmacy."

"So go," Preeti said. "I'll stay here."

"Nani told me to take you with me, so you're coming." Shay gave Preeti her best *I'm not negotiating any further* glare.

Preeti rolled her eyes. "Fine."

"I'm going to the bathroom," Shay said, turning. "When I come out, you'd better be ready."

After one night, the bathrooms adjoining the food court were an unholy mess. Crumpled paper towels overflowed from the garbage bin, and the dispenser was empty. A woman had her shirt off and was splashing water under her arms, then drying her pits with the air dryer. Another woman stepped gingerly out of a stall.

"There's no TP," she said. "And I think that one's broken." She pulled a tissue from her pocket and blew her nose loudly.

Shay thanked the woman for the tip and splashed water on her face. Looking up, she realized too late how bad an idea it had been to stand in front of a mirror. Her hair hung limp around her face. Her skin looked dull. She dared not smell her breath.

Preeti burst into the bathroom. "We're on the news!" she squealed, as if this were a good thing. "Not local, national! Fox has a little screen blurb and everything!" She ran back out.

Shay stared at her reflection for a few more seconds, a haggard face in horrific fluorescent lighting, then wiped her skin with her sleeve and prepared for the hysteria that was about to ensue.

But there was no hysteria. People crowded around the TVs in the window of the Silver Screen store calmly viewing their private nightmare like it was happening to someone else. Fox had no new information, not even news of the bomb. The newscaster just restated what the local stations had said last night. "We've learned that a security situation has led the authorities to shut down a mall in Westchester County, New York. The exact nature of the security problem has not been released, but we have learned that services have been provided to people in the mall. We will update you as we receive new information."

The only change was that Fox had a helicopter and it showed live coverage of the mall as it circled. Shay heard the telltale chopping and looked up to see the thing pass overhead. It was surreal to see your own life on TV. To be a news story. Especially when you had more information than the people on the news.

Once the program broke for commercials, people in the food court huddled around their tables—groups had pushed tables together to form little camps—and whispered. Some people began to cry. Most looked around, suddenly suspicious again of everyone else.

Shay grabbed Preeti from where she stood with her new friends. "I need contact solution," she said, dragging her across the food court toward the PhreshPharm.

"Do you think we'll get to stay here again tonight?" Preeti asked, looking up at Shay with a hopeful smile on her face.

"Get to?" Shay asked. "Yes, I believe that we shall have the privilege of sleeping on a table once again."

Preeti tucked her arms in and bounced a few happy steps. "Awesome!" she squealed. "Sahra and Lia wanted to have a sleepover in Hollister. Can we move there?"

"Whatever," Shay said. She power-walked toward the PhreshPharm, knowing how silly that was, as if they were going to sell their last contact case in the next five minutes, but she couldn't help herself. Everything felt desperate. Survival depended upon a bottle of contact solution.

It took twenty minutes round trip to get to the Phresh-Pharm and back, and in that time, the mood had grown worse in the food court. Shay found Nani at her table—still on the same Sudoku puzzle as before lunch—and showed her the meager ration of supplies she'd gotten. For ten bucks, she'd been given a bag containing a toothbrush, tiny tube of toothpaste, travel-sized deodorant, and a bar of soap. For two dollars more, they added the "contact package"—a small bottle of contact solution and case—and told her to use it sparingly. Shay felt lucky she'd gotten there before everything was gone.

"Nani?" Shay asked.

Nani touched her hand to her neck. "My throat feels like paper," she said, her voice gravelly. "Would you be so sweet as to get me some water?"

If Nani was asking for help, she must have felt truly terrible. Shay ran to the nearest water fountain and filled one of the cups the mall had provided. She brought it to her grandmother, who drank slowly.

"Thank you, sweet girl," Nani said, handing her back the cup.

"I'll get more," Shay said. The cup trembled in her hand.

"No more," Nani said. "I'll have to move into the bathroom!" She smiled a weak smile, then returned to staring at the puzzle.

Shay needed to take Nani someplace more comfortable. She slipped her toiletries into her bag and began calculating what was closest. Her first problem, though, was to round up Preeti, who had left Shay's side when they reached the edge of the food court. She'd run into the crowd of kids as if being away from her precious friends for even twenty minutes was the equivalent of a lifetime. Shay hadn't seen her friends in months.

As Shay glanced around, she noticed a mall cop speaking to some people at a table. He had a pad of paper in his hands. The people spoke to him, then pointed toward Shay.

Shay's blood ran cold. Why were they pointing at her?

She looked around and saw another cop at the other end of the food court also talking to some people at a table. They too pointed at Shay. No, not at Shay. At Nani.

The cops began weaving their way through the tables toward Shay. She froze—there was no way to escape them. The whole cafeteria space was open except for a few potted plants. Why were they coming toward her?

But then the guard stopped at another table and began talking to the people sitting there. Shay strained her ears. She heard the word *sickness*. She heard the words *acting funny*. She didn't wait to see where these next people would point.

"Nani," Shay said, grabbing her grandmother's arm. "We have to go."

"Why, dear?" Nani said. But when she saw Shay's face, she nodded and picked up her bag. She closed the Sudoku book and slipped it inside. "Where's Preeti?"

"Let's just move away from here."

When Shay was sure all eyes were elsewhere, she ducked with Nani behind the planter, then wound as casually as she could manage through the tables toward the crowds of children at the Ferris wheel. Shay said a quick prayer of thanks for how short her grandmother was—she was barely taller than the kids and thus blended right in.

Shay spotted Preeti near a vending machine kiosk talking to some girls.

"We're leaving," Shay said.

Preeti scrunched up her face like she was going to argue, but then saw Nani and went to grab her purse. Shay scanned the mall directory. Harry's was at the end of the hall, and there was a Domestic Decor on the first floor.

Then she ran her finger over the word *Grill'n'Shake*. *Marco.*

The Grill'n'Shake was just above them and near the elevator. It had padded booths. And if they were changing locations, why not move to a place where she would have someone to talk to about all this?

Preeti trotted over to the kiosk, still struggling to get the strap of her bag over her head.

"Let's move," Shay said, striding into the hallway with one arm linked through Nani's. She walked as fast as she could without dragging her grandmother outright down the tiles.

"Where are we going?" Preeti asked as she shuffled along behind Shay.

"The Grill'n'Shake."

"Fine," Preeti said, hugging her arms across her chest. "But I want to sleep in Hollister. And I get my own shake."

Shay stomped right up to the hostess station. "Table for three."

The hostess scribbled something on a paper and handed Shay a vibrating, plastic disk with blinking red lights. "When it buzzes again, come up here."

Shay gritted her teeth. She was so close to seeing Marco. *Only a few more minutes,* she told herself.

Preeti nudged her in the back. "We need to find Nani a seat," she said in a small voice.

Shay turned. Her grandmother leaned against the railing. She half smiled at Shay and waved. She'd walked too fast. *I'm an idiot!*

Taking her grandmother's arm, Shay led Nani to an empty chair in the waiting area beside the hostess stand. "Just a few minutes, Nani," she said, squeezing her hand.

"It's better here than the food court?" Nani asked, brow furrowed.

Shay scanned the crowd. There were no police officers anywhere. No fingers pointing at them. "Much better."

Preeti slumped on the floor next to Nani. "Can I have the phone?"

"Who are you calling?" Shay kept her eyes on the crowd, watching for any inquisitive officers.

"She can use it if she likes," Nani said, pulling the phone out of her bag. "The last thing I need is another call from your parents." She smiled and passed the phone to Preeti.

Preeti flipped it open. "It's dead," she said. "Do you have the charger?"

"No wonder your mother has not called since this morning," Nani said, her voice suddenly sounding concerned. It was one thing to be constantly pestered by Ba and Bapuji, and another entirely to think that they were trying to pester them but couldn't get through.

"We'll go to the mobile phone place after dinner," Shay said.

"Why are you so desperate to eat at the Grill'n'Shake?" Preeti asked, eyes squinting like she knew she was onto something. "You don't even like their fries."

Just then, Ryan—of all people, Ryan—came strolling toward the hostess stand from the dining area.

Shay was not angry. She wanted to be angry, demand

her book back and let that be the end of it, but instead all she felt was joy at seeing him again.

"Shay?" Ryan walked up to her, a smile creeping across his face.

"Hi," she said, brushing her hair behind her ear. "I guess everyone had the same idea."

He pulled her book out of his back pocket. "I really liked this," he said, placing it in her hands.

"You read it?" she asked. She hoped he couldn't see the tremble in her fingers.

He smiled. He was gorgeous. He'd read her book. "I didn't have much else to do last night," he said.

"Yo! J. Shrimp!" Some huge guy waved at Ryan from halfway down the hall.

Ryan waved back. "I have to go," he said. "But I want to talk to you about it. The book. I mean, if you want."

Her heart began to pound in her chest. *Yes, I want!*

"Sure," she said. "We could meet at Baxter's Books."

"I'll call you," he said, turning. Then he stopped. "Wait, I lost my phone."

Shay shrugged. "Mine's dead anyway."

"So we'll meet by the registers. Nine o'clock tomorrow?" He began shuffling away backward toward his friends. He looked hopeful, as if he really did want to meet her. As if this wasn't all some hallucination on her part.

"Nine on the dot!" she shouted, waving. Like an idiot. She felt ready to float away.

"So *that's* why we had to come to the Grill'n'Shake," Preeti said, her lips pursed in a smug smile.

Even Nani had a mischievous look on her face. "I think you owe your grandmother some kind of explanation," Nani said. Then she coughed and the sparkle of the healthy grandmother Shay used to have disappeared.

The plastic disk buzzed.

"Let's get you some more water," Shay said.

Nani leaned on both Shay and Preeti as they wound their way into the restaurant.

MARCO

After Mike the Moron left, Marco went back to his stakeout. The government must have thought everyone in the mall was an idiot—of course, they'd been right. No one except Marco seemed to have noticed the plywood walls erected overnight around the former PaperClips. Then again, no one else except the girl from the police cruiser knew about the bomb.

Marco had started his hunt for information as soon as he got a break from the breakfast rush. The plywood wall was a dead giveaway; the only question was how to spy on the place without getting caught. He employed a tried and true method he'd used as a kid to eavesdrop on his sisters. He bought a cheap baby monitor and installed the baby end under a discarded bag at the edge of the plywood wall, mic facing the crack. So far, back in the restaurant, he'd heard very little, but what little he'd heard was fascinating.

". . . air samples within the ducts have yielded no information . . ."

". . . if there's anthrax, I want the cops in gloves . . ." *The senator.*

From this, he gleaned that (a) the government had no idea what they were dealing with and (b) they assumed it was a deadly biotoxin. Meaning everyone located where the contaminated air duct let out was royally screwed. At least anthrax wasn't contagious.

"Carvajal!" Mr. Seveglia's hand waved Marco into the manager's cramped office. "Can I sign you up for an extra shift?"

Marco switched off the monitor, hid the receiver in the bottom of the host stand, and approached. "Of course, sir," he said. He could use the extra cash, given that he needed a new bike thanks to Mike the Moron.

"My man," Mr. Seveglia said, patting Marco on the arm.

Of course, the extra work would cut into his stakeout time. He needed a map of the ventilation system. Maybe if he broke into the janitorial offices during his next break . . .

"Marco." It was Trish, the bitchy hostess.

"Patricia."

"Some girl at table fifteen asked for you."

This was unprecedented. Marco was not good with people. Especially his peers. His peers tended to be assholes.

He glanced around the corner and saw that table fifteen was occupied by an old lady, a little kid, and the girl from the police cruiser. *Shay.*

Last night he'd blathered on like some drunk moron.

Now she expected him to talk with her again. He sighed. At least she was pretty.

He stalked over to her bench seat. "You wanted to talk?"

She looked relieved to see him. "Marco, right?"

Her grandmother said something in a foreign language—not Spanish. The little girl laughed. Shay blushed and made a face at the little girl—Marco assumed that they were sisters.

"Sorry," Shay said. "My grandmother doesn't speak any English." She seemed to brace herself slightly, as if she'd borne the brunt of sarcastic comments at her grandmother's lack of fluency. Perhaps they had more in common than Marco had thought.

"My grandmother's lived here for thirty years and speaks less than ten words of English," he said.

Shay's face brightened. "So you know what it's like?"

"Shopping with her outside of her neighborhood in the Bronx can be described as a cultural experience at best." Marco ventured a smile. He was not attractive—his sisters had dubbed him scarecrow for his lankiness, and his mother often said that he'd grow into his features, meaning *sorry you're hideous now*—but he looked better when he smiled.

"So how did you two meet?" the sister asked in a sing-songy, playground-taunt voice. Marco responded viscerally to the tone.

"Can you show me where the bathrooms are?" Shay interjected, eyes flicking toward the sign like she knew where they were and just wanted to get away from the table.

"This way," Marco said, stepping as far from the sister as possible.

"Running off with yet *another* boy?" the sister mocked.

Shay flashed her sister a withering glare and followed Marco around the corner. Once hidden from her family's view, she slumped into the nearest empty chair and dropped her head onto the tabletop.

"How can you seem so normal?" she said. "Knowing what we know." Her voice was muffled by her folded arms.

"What, that we're caught in a death trap?"

Shay glanced up at Marco like he'd bitten her. He decided to holster his usual mode of response. He wanted to talk to this girl.

"Having the job makes it easier," he said, sitting opposite her. "Keeps my mind off things." He would not say anything about his spy operation.

"My job isn't helping me at all." She waved her hand up, then let it flop back onto her arm.

"Job?" Marco asked.

"Taking care of my grandmother and sister," Shay said. "My grandmother's diabetic. She needs insulin shots. And my sister is just, well." Shay looked at him, eyebrows raised. "You have a little sister?"

"I'm the little brother, so you'll get no sympathy from me."

Shay smiled and in that moment, Marco would have sworn that she was the prettiest girl he had ever seen—in magazines, movies, anywhere.

"There were cops in the food court asking about sick people," she continued. "Have the cops come through here?"

"No cops," Marco said. He hadn't seen a cop since being let out of the squad car. The four guys who first arrived on the scene had grilled him for a few hours, but had finally accepted that Marco was not some lone bomber looking for publicity by ratting out his own terrorist attack.

"People pointed at my grandmother," Shay said. She stared at the wall. "I had to get her away from there. Why are the cops asking about sick people?"

"I'm sure it's nothing," Marco said, trying to bring back that glowing smile. "The cops were probably just making a routine check." He didn't want to upset her more by telling her that if it was anthrax, Grandma would be dead in forty-eight hours.

"Yeah," she said, obsessively running her nail across the table. "I guess. But we *are* being quarantined; that means something."

"The cops are just covering their collective ass. They'll let us out soon." An awkward silence descended. "You go to West Nyack?" he asked, taking a stab into the discursive darkness.

"No, Stonecliff."

"I didn't think so," he said. "I'd have noticed you."

Shay gave him a raised-eyebrow look like she could smell him coming from a mile away. Was he actually flirting?

"You like it there?" he said.

"We just moved here," she said. "Figures I move somewhere just in time to end up in a terrorist attack. Do you think whoever did it is still in the mall?"

"Sure. The guy probably planted the bomb, then went shoe shopping." He just couldn't turn off the sarcasm—

Shay did not look amused. He forged ahead. "Where'd you move from?"

"Jersey," she said, without adding more. "Why hasn't the bomb blown up already?"

"Maybe it did and we're all dead," he said.

"Heaven's a bit of a disappointment."

"Yeah, and the food sucks."

She smiled. She got his gallows humor. He felt suddenly grateful for having been trapped in the squad car for all of yesterday.

"I can't believe we're joking about this," she said, sounding more relieved than angry.

"Ha!" he said in a fake accent. "I laugh in the face of death!" He felt giddy, talking so much.

"I knew it," she said. "You're a theater nerd."

"Film nerd," he corrected. "Different species entirely."

"Too bad." She flipped her hair, exposing the faded brown lines of leaves curving around her collarbone. "I'm a theater nerd."

He felt a great urge to run his fingertips along the lines of those leaves. "Maybe we're not so different after all." It took all the forces of his will to keep from touching her.

The mall speaker beeped and it was announced that cots were available in the open spaces of the first floor. Marco wondered if Shay might be more comfortable bunking in a booth with him. He wondered how to broach the offer.

"Shaila!"

The sister's voice shattered the moment. Shay jumped from her chair, banging her knee, and bolted around the corner. Marco followed. The grandmother was slumped forward in her seat. Shay slid in beside her and began rubbing her shoulder. She mumbled something in her language, but that old lady did not need to talk. If it really was diabetes, she needed insulin. Or juice. Frida had diabetes, so Marco knew it was one of the two.

Marco ran into the kitchen and poured some OJ from the dispenser. He brought it back to the table.

"See if she needs juice," he said, pushing Nani upright. The skin over her cheekbones was dark as if it were bruised.

Shay leaned back, allowing him to reach over and dribble juice into Grandma's slack mouth. Nothing.

"Why isn't it working?" the sister whined.

Time for Plan B.

Marco stood on a chair. "Excuse me!" he shouted. "There is a patron in this restaurant in need of insulin. Does anyone have insulin?"

The room went silent. People looked at each other like they weren't sure whether insulin was a bad thing to have. When some people refused to look at him, he decided those were the ones who probably had it. He hopped off the chair and raced to the nearest coward.

"If you have insulin, give it to me." He pointed to where Shay sat with her grandmother. "That woman could die."

The man hunched his shoulders over his triple-decker burger. "I don't have any insulin, so bug off."

Marco felt the old anger well up inside. He knew this guy had insulin. The jerk just wouldn't help.

Before he had a chance to explode all over this asshole, a young woman stepped forward. "Here," she said, handing him a vial and needle. "I got some this morning from the guards."

Marco took a deep breath. "Thanks," he said. He looked down at the jerk, who was stuffing a bite of burger into his mouth. "At least some people aren't entirely selfish."

He raced back to Shay's table. "Get up!" he shouted. Shay slid out of his way. Marco jammed the needle into the bottle and withdrew the dose Frida took—he had no idea what this old lady's scrip said, but hell if they had a lot of time to figure that out.

Marco knelt next to the old lady, lifted the flimsy fabric of her wrap, and jammed the needle into her upper arm. He watched her face, waiting for a sign that she'd revived. But then someone grabbed his shoulders and pulled him away from the woman.

Marco was dropped into the next booth by a person— man, woman, who knew?—in a blue, plastic hazmat suit. Some people in the restaurant screamed. Marco glanced around for where Shay was. She and her sister were being held by two security guards.

"Everyone, stay calm," the hazmat person said, sounding disturbingly like Darth Vader. "I am from a federal emergency medical team. We will evacuate this woman for treatment."

A fork dropped onto a plate. Otherwise, the room was silent. Marco was fairly sure everyone's brains were processing the same thought: Why was a dude in a hazmat suit in the Grill'n'Shake? But Marco knew exactly why this person was in a suit. He was from the Outside; he had not been contaminated by the bomb.

Shay screamed. "No!" She wriggled in the guard's grasp. "She's just diabetic!"

A guard rolled in a gurney and, with the others' help, hefted the grandmother onto it. They pushed it down the aisle and out of the restaurant. Shay and her sister stumbled, sobbing, after them.

Once the medical team cleared the entryway, people went back to eating as if nothing had happened. Amazing, the herd's ability to forget the disturbance of their peace. Some patrons even congratulated Marco on saving the old lady's life. How blind were they? Grandma's life was far from saved—exactly how far was the mystery in need of solving.

Marco found Mr. Seveglia in the kitchen interrogating the line cook about supplies.

"Sir?" Marco asked. "The girl who left with that old lady is a friend. Can I go see what happened to her?"

Mr. Seveglia glanced up at the clock above the freezer door. "We got the dinner rush starting in five," he said. "Get your tables cleaned and ready. You can find her when you're done with your shift."

Marco felt that anger inside him once more, but tamped it down. He couldn't blow up at the manager. He needed his job. He'd try to find Shay after closing, around eleven. It wasn't like she could go anywhere.

DAY
— THREE —
· MONDAY ·

R
Y
A
N

Ryan ran all the way to Baxter's Books, that's how much he wanted to see Shay. He'd started at a walk, but as he thought of her, of getting to spend a whole day in her presence, he'd ended up taking the stairs two at a time up the escalator and burst, breathless and smiling, into the wet coffee stink of the bookstore. Now he had twenty minutes to kill. He decided to check if they stocked any Tagore.

It hadn't been easy ditching Mike and Drew. Mike had become a bit of a tyrant after the three of them had been stalked by the Tarrytown guys for all of yesterday evening. Lucky for Ryan, it was announced at Lights On that stations had been set up at three locations in the mall for people to register to have their places of employment or schools notified of their detainment. Knowing Mike and Drew would never volunteer to be put on a government list, Ryan had the perfect excuse to escape alone. Mike had told Ryan to put his name on the list and get his ass back to the Abercrombie.

"I promised your brother I'd watch out for you," he said, holding up his phone. Mike had texted Thad about the situation and that he and Drew had things under control.

"I feel extremely watched out for," Ryan had said as he left.

One entire bookshelf was devoted to Rabindranath Tagore. There were books of essays, letters, novels, stories, and some giant thing called *The Oxford Tagore Translations*. Ryan pulled out the smallest, least-intimidating paperback. It flipped open to a weird-looking poem called "Palm-tree." Ryan liked the simplicity of the thing. The tree thought about flying when the wind blew through it, but when the wind stopped, the tree remembered it was stuck in the dirt and was cool with that.

Ryan understood that tree. Here, in the thick silence between the bookshelves, he could read poetry, he could dream of having a girl like Shay. Out there, he had to stay focused. He could date girls, but only the safe ones, the ones who didn't ask for too much, who could be fit between practices and games. He'd only spent a half hour with Shay, but already he knew she was anything but safe, and yet she was all that he wanted.

The store speaker beeped. "Will Ryan please come to the information desk."

She's here. Ryan left the book on the shelf and ran for the information desk. "I'm Ryan," he said, glancing around to see where she'd gone. The guy behind the counter handed him the phone. It was Shay.

"I'm sorry I'm calling late," she said.

Ryan hadn't even noticed. "No problem," he said. "I found some more Tagore."

"He's the best," Shay said, her last word stretching into a yawn. She continued, "I can't meet you today. My grandmother—she has diabetes and is in the infirmary."

Ryan slumped against the counter. "Oh, that's rough," he said. He tried to sound like he cared more about her grandmother's welfare than the fact that she wasn't going to meet him. He didn't think he'd succeeded.

"I'm sorry," she said.

"No, hey," he said, too fast. "No problem. I'll catch you some other time."

She didn't say anything for a moment. "Yeah," she said. "I guess we can't get away from each other."

"No," he said. He felt like if their conversation were a car, it had turned onto the wrong street.

"I've got to go," she said. "Bye."

She hung up before he could think of anything to say. Ryan handed the phone back to the guy. "Thanks," he said.

He was not sure what had just happened, but it hadn't been good.

Whenever Ryan felt bad, he liked to rock climb. Something about the experience of relying on his own muscles, of hanging far above everyone else, calmed whatever confusion swirled around inside him. Like when his parents fought. When they started to get into it with each other,

Ryan instantly got onto his bike and rode to the climbing gym.

Like now. He needed to be on the wall. He hoped the sales guys at Shep's were still letting people up.

Just outside Baxter's, across from the Grill'n'Shake, a cop and a person in a hazmat suit sat behind a table. There was no sign on the table, just what looked like a tackle box, a metal case full of vials, and an empty chair next to the hazmat guy. Ryan walked on the opposite side of the hall as he passed.

The mall speakers squealed.

"Patrons of the Shops at Stonecliff, stations have been established throughout the mall staffed by members of the security team. Some of these individuals are wearing plastic suits for their and your own safety. Please do not be alarmed by the suits.

"You are asked to make your way to the nearest station for a blood test. Everyone must get tested. The police officers at each station have a list of all the people in the mall as compiled on the first evening of the security situation. You must be marked as having completed the testing before you will be allowed to leave the mall. Thank you for your cooperation."

Ryan didn't trust this for a second. He speed-walked down the hall, away from what he now realized was a testing station. He wanted as much distance between himself and the hazmat guy as possible. He had to climb; when he'd calmed down, he'd find the guys. They would know what to do.

Racing away from one testing station only brought him closer to another—they were set up everywhere. And now security guards patrolled the halls in groups of two. Ryan passed a man who began coughing up a lung. A pair of guards was on him in a second.

Ryan ran to Shep's, stopping only once he was inside the doorway. He bent over a weight bench display to catch his breath. The climbing wall was at the back. Thankfully, it looked like they were letting people up and still had the auto belay devices running for solos.

"Well, look what just fell into our laps," a voice snarled from down the aisle.

Ryan checked over his shoulder and saw two of the Tarrytown linemen striding toward him. He was about to bolt for the door when a hand caught him around the back of the neck. "We have some unfinished business."

They dragged Ryan out into the hall, and steered him toward a narrow hallway labeled "Staff Only." He knew he should scream. But what kind of loser screams for help in the middle of a mall?

The guy holding his neck threw him forward, and Ryan thrust his hands in front of himself to keep from smashing against a metal door. He flipped over to face them.

"You West Nyack assholes are always strutting around like you're so great," one of them said. He feinted at Ryan's head; Ryan blocked high; the kid nailed him in the gut.

Ryan doubled over. He'd never been punched before. Sacked, tackled, but not punched. The pain was exquisite.

"He doesn't look so great now," another grunted.

A foot connected with his face, dropping Ryan to his butt. He held his head to keep it from fracturing apart.

"Asswipe's not even defending himself," another said.

Ryan was pulled to his feet. A drop of blood fell from his nose, marking the tile. He lifted his eyes.

"Put your hands up, you pussy," the first snarled, bouncing slightly like some sort of boxer. "I guess Thad's the only one with balls in your family."

Ryan wiped the back of his hand under his nose, leaving a trail of bright red across his skin. "I don't want to fight," he said. Blood dripped down his throat. After ten years of football, he was used to the taste.

"No one cares what you want," the guy said.

He threw another punch at Ryan's face. Ryan expected it this time and blocked. He ducked and drove his shoulder into the guy, pushing him against the other three. If he could push them down the hall, he could break free at the main corridor.

"Get around him!" another shouted.

Arms encircled Ryan's chest, lifting him away from his target. One arm pulled back and punched him in the kidney. A knee connected with his groin, and Ryan collapsed forward. The guy let him flop onto the tile. They were all laughing. One gave him a final kick in the stomach. Then they left.

Ryan allowed himself a few minutes to lie curled on the floor. He'd expected a fight to be more like practice—brutal, but not terrible. He'd forgotten the power of padding, the simple safety of a cup. It made him think of the time his father punched his mother. Ryan had not understood the pain involved. The violation. But Thad had gone ballistic and driven Dad's car into a tree. Apparently, Thad had understood.

Standing, he forced himself not to cry, but water slicked his cheeks nonetheless. He wiped his face on his shirt, which he thanked god was navy so the blood didn't stand out too much. He managed a shambling walk down the hall. He prayed Mike and Drew were still in Abercrombie.

The store was dark as usual, but Ryan spotted Mike in a pool of light shoving Sportade bottles and PowerBars into a backpack.

"Shrimp," Mike said, seeing Ryan's silhouette approach. "We gathered some food in case of shortages."

Ryan stumbled forward, leaning on a rack of sweatshirts. "Tarrytown," he muttered. "Assholes cornered me."

Mike dropped the bag and caught Ryan's shirt, lowered him to the floor and helped him to lean against the wall.

"What happened?" Mike said.

Ryan told him. Mike's face was stony. His eyes became harder, fiercer with each word.

"Bonner," Mike snarled at a dark corner. "Drop the chick. There are some gentlemen in need of a lesson in manners."

Bonner emerged from the shadows, adjusting himself and zipping his fly. He caught a glimpse of Ryan's face, which must have looked about as bad as Ryan felt.

"Where are they?" Drew said.

Ryan would not stay behind. He followed Mike and Drew through the halls as they trolled for the Tarrytown guys. They found the four dunking baskets at a game in the arcade. Drew ripped a fake shotgun out of the neighboring game and smashed three of them in the back of their heads, dropping them like rocks. Mike sucker-punched the other guy in the back, then grabbed his hair and wheeled him around to face Ryan.

"Do you see what you did?" he whispered into the kid's hair.

The Tarrytown kid looked at Ryan. "Got your boys to come to your defense?" he taunted.

Ryan took the plastic shotgun from Drew and smashed the kid in the face with the butt. The kid screamed. Blood shot from his nose, which lay at an odd angle to his face. Satisfaction calmed Ryan's body; at the same time, fear bubbled up. *Did I just break his nose?*

"What the hell, Richter?" The kid's voice sounded wet with blood.

Mike smashed the kid's head into the wall of a video game. "You mess with my family," he said, "you mess with me." He let the kid drop to the floor. "And my team is my family, got it, Martin?"

The other three began to push themselves to standing. Drew nailed all three in the gut and they fell back to the floor.

"Stay, dirtbags," he said.

The manager of the arcade yelled for the cops and Mike cocked his head like it was time to go.

"Hope you've learned your lesson," Mike said. He put a shoulder under Ryan's arm and helped him out of the arcade.

Mike patted the manager on the shoulder as he passed. "Sorry about the mess."

The manager shrank back. That was the power of Mike—no one messed with him.

Drew seemed invigorated. He bounced on his feet as he walked, then turned to a random woman and screamed in her face, causing her to run shrieking in the opposite direction. Drew laughed and punched the air.

A hazmat dude stepped out of the crowd, stared at Drew, then waved for a nearby mall cop.

Mike smacked Drew in the back of the head. "Chill."

Drew dialed it down and tried to blend in. They reached the escalator and rode down toward the Abercrombie.

Mike leaned Ryan against the railing, checked to see if the mall cop had followed. "I think it's time we check in with Taco about our exit strategy."

Ryan had no idea what the dish kid had to do with an exit, but he was willing to go along with any strategy if it meant getting out of this rat cage.

SHAY

Shay stroked Preeti's head, which lay in her lap. Ever since their arrival yesterday at the emergency medical center, they'd been told to wait on folding chairs beside the glass front wall of what had once been a PaperClips. From the tinny beat thumping out of the headphones, Shay could tell Preeti was listening to Shay's dance mix, made for her birthday party last spring. Ba had agreed to let Shay invite the whole theater company over. They played a game of Pictionary on a wipe board filched from Bapuji's office, then turned on this silly spinning light thing Shweta had brought and had a massive dance party in the living room. When Shay escaped onto the back deck to get a breath of fresh air, Raj Patel had kissed her. It'd been nothing special, but nice anyway.

Her family should never have moved. So what if Ba got a whole department to run at this new hospital? If they had stayed in Edison, Shay would never have dragged Nani to the mall on a Saturday—she would have gone with Shweta or Kaitlyn. Nani would have been home, safe.

If only the stupid hazmat doctors would talk to her. Every time she poked her head through the wall of curtain—which delineated the meager waiting area at the front of the ex-PaperClips from the actual medical part of the emergency medical center—she was told that someone would be with her shortly and would she please sit back down. She had been sitting on this folding chair for more than twelve hours—clearly "shortly" meant something different to these hazmat people.

It was Preeti who'd reminded her about the date with Ryan. "Isn't one of your boyfriends waiting for you in a bookstore?" she'd asked. Shay had completely forgotten. She'd bolted across to the Domestic Decor, snuck over to an abandoned sales desk, and called the bookstore to cancel. No way she was leaving that medical center without Nani. At this point, however—some seventeen hours after their arrival, now that she was looking at her watch—Shay was beginning to suspect the hazmat people would never consent to Nani's removal from their clutches.

A pair of security guards tromped through the plastic covering the former PaperClips' doorway. Between them, an old woman stumbled on shaking legs. She began to cough loud, hacking coughs. She slipped from the guards' grasp and fell to the floor, still coughing.

Her ears were blue. Somehow, all Shay could focus on were the ears. They looked like something off a Halloween mask. The guards hefted the woman back to her feet and dragged her behind the curtain. Shay listened to the coughing as it drifted back through the space beyond the Wall of Curtain.

"That lady seems pretty sick," Preeti said.

She did. And not normal sick. Shay hadn't allowed herself to think too much about why the hell members of the medical team were in hazmat suits. In the parking garage, she'd heard the senator say something about anthrax. Had the bomb exposed them to anthrax?

No. That was paranoid thinking. She felt fine. If there was anthrax somewhere, she would not feel fine. But what if old blue-ears was contagious? She had to get Nani out of this place.

Shay held open the main curtain door for Preeti.

"There's just more curtain," Preeti said. "How are we going to find Nani?"

Shay peeked behind the nearest curtain. "Trial and error."

A machine started beeping madly somewhere near the back of the vast curtain complex. Several hazmat people swept aside a neighboring curtain, pushed past Shay and Preeti, and rushed to the source. They hadn't even noticed the two infiltrators. This was Shay's chance.

Each curtain-room contained two cots, most only one person. On the fourth try, Shay found Nani lying down, looking up at the sliver of sky visible over the top of the curtain wall through the windowed front of the Paper-Clips. If Nani was awake, whatever diabetes crisis she'd suffered had to be over. Shay grabbed Preeti by the arm and dragged her swiftly into the room.

"Nani?" Shaila asked, kneeling beside the cot.

Nani covered her face with her sari and coughed. "Sweet girl," Nani said, pushing herself up.

"I'm getting you out of here," Shay said.

Nani nodded. "This is not a good place."

The beeping became a steady, high-pitched drone, then ceased. The tops of two hazmat suits drifted past the curtain that led to the main hall; Shay heard the scratchy voices of the medical people inside say "flatlined."

That old lady died?

Nani slipped her feet over the side of the cot. She coughed again. But her ears were brown—the right color. She did not have whatever that other old lady had. She was not going to die.

More hazmat suits were visible outside of their curtain-room. Shay would not be able to sneak Nani out the way she and Preeti had come in.

Shay began peeking behind the other three curtain-walls. The two side walls bordered other curtained rooms, but the back curtain hung a few inches from the windowed exterior wall, and that narrow span of floor ran from where Shay stood all the way to the front of the store.

Shay swept aside the back curtain. "Nani, come hide behind here," she whispered.

Nani looked at Shay, confused. "Dear one, you think they won't notice us hiding?"

Shay smiled wickedly. "Not if we sneak to the front of this place and out the door, they won't."

Preeti bounced up. "Yes," she said, grabbing Nani's arm. "Come on, Nani."

Shay stood in front of Nani, and Preeti took up the

rear. With their backs pressed against the windows, they walked on tiptoes with stomachs sucked in along the wall of the PaperClips. They passed beyond their room's curtain to that of the one next to it. The person in that room—a woman, judging by the voice—was talking to someone.

"I just have a cold," she said. "The guy in the suit brought me here without even asking why I was coughing."

"That was protocol." Another woman's voice. Shay recognized it—it was the senator she'd seen on the first night in the parking garage. The senator continued, "We're testing everyone, but I've asked the staff to bring anyone who seems sick here for more private treatment."

I've asked . . . Shay realized that the senator was running this show. The same senator who'd screwed up and gotten them all quarantined.

In the next curtain-room, the person—a man—was shouting. "I want out of here, right now!" he bellowed.

Suddenly, an elbow pierced through the curtains, smashing into the wall of the PaperClips and barely missing Nani's head. Her eyes went wide with shock and Shay slapped her hand over her own mouth to remind Nani not to scream. Preeti's face crumpled as if about to break into a sob. Silent tears trickled down her cheeks.

The elbow was dragged back through the curtain wall. A muffled voice from one of the hazmat masks shouted, "Sedate him!" The man kicked the curtain, nailing Shay in the shin. She clamped her jaws to keep from screaming—he'd hit her good and hard. There'd be a mega bruise. Then the foot dropped onto the tile and slid back under the curtain. From the sounds of men grunting and metal squealing, the man was being wrestled onto a cot.

Shay cocked her head and shuffled forward, limping slightly now. Her left leg throbbed from the blow. She bit the inside of her cheek to stay focused.

The curtains ended ten feet from the front wall of the PaperClips. Shay peeked around the edge and saw that the only person in the waiting area was a guy about her age. He stared vacantly at the Wall of Curtain. Shay waved to Nani and Preeti and stepped quickly out into the waiting area.

The boy looked up. He seemed surprised. Shay froze, afraid he'd give them away. *Please,* she mouthed, holding a finger to her lips.

The kid nodded, then went back to staring at the curtains. He understood. She wondered if she should tell him about the space between the curtain and the wall, in case he needed it in the near future.

"What are we waiting for?" Preeti whispered, taking her arm. "Let's get out of here."

Shay nodded and took Nani's hand.

They walked slowly, casually out of the PaperClips, then through the plywood door and into the hall. Though Shay wanted to run as fast as possible away from that place, she didn't want to draw any unwanted attention, so they walked at a snail's pace down the short corridor. Once they reached the main hall, there were more people. Shay risked moving at a fast trot all the way to the other end of the mall.

Shay had decided upon the inflatable mattress store, SnoozeSelect, because first, she'd never seen anyone shopping in it before, and second, there would be lots of full-sized beds for Nani to rest on. When they arrived at its entry, Shay noticed that no one—neither shopper nor salesperson—was inside. It was a lucky break—now Nani had a private bedroom down a corridor, off the main passageway, on the second floor, far from the senator's prying eyes.

Nani was breathing heavily.

"Let's get you resting on one of these," Shay said, taking her grandmother's arm and leading her to the bed farthest from the door.

Nani patted her hand. "You're so good to me," she said. "I will have to show you my secret store of henna."

Shay pressed her fingers to her chest in mock astonishment. "You have a secret henna store you haven't told me about?"

Nani leaned back into the pillows, smiling. "I have many secrets I have yet to tell you," she said. "I thought this was why you kept trying to save me from death."

Shay smiled, more because her grandmother was trying to make a joke than at the joke itself.

"What Snooze Setting are you?" Shay asked, picking up the remote. She pushed a button and a machine began pumping air into the mattress.

Nani's eyes widened and she gripped the sides of the bed. "What will they think of next?"

Shay handed her the remote and left Nani to play with the settings. Preeti remained by the door, fingers wrapped around the door frame. Shay placed a hand on Preeti's shoulder and she jumped.

"There's a table down there," Preeti said, pointing at the end of the hall where the corridor met the main passage. "There's a space-suited guy and a security guard sitting at it."

Shay watched people line up in front of the table. It was one of the testing stations mentioned in the morning announcement. One by one, the ex-shoppers sat in the chair next to the hazmat person. Each one had some blood drawn, and the vial of blood was placed in a metal box at the hazmat person's feet. The security guard checked something off on his list—the person's name, if the announcement was to be believed.

Shay and Preeti stared at the operation for a few minutes. Shay wondered if it would have been better to have just stayed in the medical ward. *Have I screwed up yet another thing?*

A little boy sat in the chair at the testing station. His mother stood behind him, hands gripping the plastic back. The boy coughed. The hazmat man looked up. The boy coughed again. The security guard lifted a walkie-talkie to his lips.

A man—the boy's father, it seemed—stepped forward and put one hand on his son's shoulder, the other around his wife. When the hazmat man stood, the father picked his kid up and tried to leave. Two more security guards appeared from down the main hallway, behind the family. The mother punched at them and the father tried to run, boy under his arm like a sack of laundry. The guards grabbed the father and boy, who was crying. The first security guard came behind the mother, who was still attacking the two holding her family, and Tasered her in the back. She slumped into the guard's arms.

The other people in the line screamed and began pushing at each other to get away from the table. Shay's knuckles were white where she gripped the door frame.

Preeti buried her face into Shay's armpit.

Something terrible was going on in this mall. Shay just had to keep Preeti and Nani safe. Hide them until this—whatever it was—was over. If she could do that, everything would be fine.

M
A
R
C
O

Someone had discovered Marco's baby monitor. When he turned the receiver on, it started beeping, which he knew from experience meant he'd been found out. Now he would have to examine the PaperClips personally if he wanted to know what had happened with Shay and her grandmother, or the senator for that matter.

The only problem was how to convince Seveglia to let him leave. There'd been some desertions in the ranks of the Grill'n'Shake staff, leading the manager to become suspicious of any and all break requests. He should have known he had nothing to fear from Marco—he needed this job and he had no desire to mingle with the gangs of kids aimlessly wandering the halls.

One of the older dishwashers had developed a cough. Marco decided to check up on him. Roberto sat in a back corner on a stool. He held a well-used handkerchief in his hand.

"Cold?" Marco asked in Spanish.

"It's sleeping in the damned kitchen," Roberto said. "They could at least give us beds."

"I could take you to the emergency medical team that was in here last night."

"Like the boss would give us the time off," Roberto said, smiling wryly.

Marco held up a finger and went into Mr. Seveglia's office. "Sir?"

The manager, who was beginning to look pretty worn out himself, took off his reading glasses and rubbed his eyes. "You got a problem, Carvajal?"

"It's not me, sir," Marco said. "Roberto isn't feeling great and I think it would be best to get him out of the kitchen. We can't afford to have any of the remaining staff get sick."

Mr. Seveglia squinted at Marco as if probing his soul for the truth of the statement. Then he put the glasses back on and turned to his computer. "You take him down and bring him back," Mr. Seveglia said. "No funny business."

Marco nodded and ducked out. He gave Roberto the thumbs-up. The old man looked shocked, but stood and followed Marco out of the kitchen.

Outside of the Grill'n'Shake, the mall was bedlam. The older folks and families tended to stay in the stores during the day, only coming out at mealtimes or to use the bathrooms, and what few security guards there were seemed to only be interested in the sick. This left the halls and open spaces to the kids, and they were taking full advantage. If Marco had felt uncomfortable in high school, this situation was like the worst-case school scenario on steroids.

"Get off my escalator!" some jerk taunted.

"Yeah, get your illegal asses back to Mexico!"

Roberto glanced at the kids, a look of concern on his face. "Is no one even trying to keep them in line?"

"They didn't throw anything," Marco replied, stepping off the escalator. "I would say they're practically restrained." He would finish this recon mission, then get his ass back into the restaurant.

The hall with the PaperClips was short and out of the way, so it was mostly empty. A guy rummaged through a trash bin near the corner off the main hall. As Marco passed, he emerged with a discarded fast-food bag.

"Lunch," the guy said to himself.

Marco noted that the Pancake Palace, which stood behind the Dumpster diver, was now mysteriously closed, its windows papered over during the night from the inside. Since the restaurant bordered the PaperClips, Marco assumed the emergency medical people had expanded their domain. *But why?*

"Where are we going?" Roberto asked as they neared the blocked exits.

Marco tapped the door in the plywood wall. "Right this way," he said.

Marco pulled open the door, allowing Roberto to step in first.

"Halt!"

Marco remained hidden behind the door.

"This area is restricted." The voice sounded distorted. It must have been an Outsider in a mask.

"Doctor?" Roberto asked in English.

"Dr. Chen!" the voice called.

Roberto began protesting in Spanish. "The kid told me you were medical people. I have a cold. Get your hands off of me!"

The voices moved away, beyond Marco's hearing. *At least he'll see a doctor . . .*

So there was no going in this door. *Where else could the senator be?* He recalled her mentioning something about the Apple Store during his confinement in the squad car. Perhaps she was using the Apple Store as a base of operations? It was also on the first floor and would have Internet access. He decided to check it out.

Though the senator was absent, the Apple Store was clearly the center of something. Near the back of the store, a rotund man with a badge dangling from his pocket—some mall official—conferred with a man sitting at a desk with three different screens on it. The two were reviewing a thick stack of papers. From the handwriting and generally wrinkled state of the paper, those must have been the lists of people trapped in the mall.

A girl in a hoodie sat under a computer table. In her lap was what appeared to be a walkie-talkie, but upon closer examination turned out to be a police scanner. Marco pretended to check out a nearby camera to better observe her. She clearly knew something was up. And she looked a bit like the senator, so he guessed she was her kid. He remembered the senator mentioning something about a kid.

The girl suddenly dropped the scanner. It clattered to the floor. The man—*her father?*—stood and asked if she was all right. She waved him off, then stood, checked something on the computer, and walked out of the store. *What did she hear?*

Marco had to talk to this girl. He'd gotten halfway down the hall after her when the guy who'd been with Richter and Bonner came running toward him. From the multi-colored bruise that was now his face, Marco guessed he'd taken a trip through a trash compactor.

"Hey, Marco!" he shouted.

That's new, Marco thought. *A Richterite who uses my given name.*

"What do you want?" Marco said, not stopping.

The guy trotted to his side. "We've been looking for you," he said.

"How lucky for me," Marco said, feigning surprise. "News flash: I don't want to see you or your best pal Mike."

"Is this about yesterday?" the kid said. "Mike said you dinged his car, but he seems to be taking it way hard."

Marco stopped and gave this guy the once-over. "What happened to your face?"

The kid brushed back his shaggy brown hair. "Doesn't matter," he said. "We need your help."

Marco wondered if the face was Richter's doing. "What makes Richter think I'd help him?"

"Because we want to escape."

The word *escape* caught Marco's interest. There would

be no need to figure out what was wrong with the mall if he was no longer in it. "What makes you think I know how to escape the mall?" he said.

"You know the service halls and stuff," the guy said, waving his hand like Marco ran some black-market operation. "Look, you don't have to help us, but this place is not safe." He adjusted his shirt, wincing as if his own skin were painful to him. "You might want some people watching out for you. If you help us, we'll have your back."

"Not once you get out of here you won't," Marco said.

"Well, if we get out, you won't need your back watched because we'll be out." He shuffled on his feet. "We just want to see if there's a way to escape."

Marco thought about whether there could be any unguarded exit. The loading docks had to be watched—they were the obvious escape routes. And he'd seen on his last garbage run that all the parking garage entrance ramps were blocked with airtight barriers. But there was an old fire escape out of the parking garage level in the service hallway that might be obscure enough to have been forgotten. It was down a little side hall and was just a hatch in the ceiling. Maybe that was unlocked? *Perhaps I can find Shay and help her out of here?*

"Why would I show you an escape route when I can just go there myself, without you?" Marco said.

"Because I'd skin you alive." Fleshy hands plopped down on Marco's shoulders. *Bonner.*

"You wouldn't be holding out on us, would you, Taco?" Mike said, slinking up from behind Drew.

Having already implied the existence of an escape route, outright denial seemed impossible or at least the move most likely to result in a punch to the face. The better plan was balls-out confidence.

"I might have an idea of how to escape," Marco said, rolling his shoulders and shrugging off Drew's grasp. "But I want something in return for showing it to you."

Drew cracked his knuckles. "You don't seem to be in too great a bargaining position, Mallrat."

"I have an escape plan, and you don't," Marco said, crossing his arms over his chest, trying to look a bit braver than he felt. "So, yeah, I'm in a fairly good bargaining position."

Mike's eyes squinted down to slivers. "All right, Taco," he said. "What are your terms?"

"First," he said. "It's Marco. And second, you give up trying to kill me." This would be his insurance policy: In case he survived the killer air in the mall, he would not have to worry about being murdered by Mike at school.

Mike lifted his eyebrows. "Whoa," he said. "That's steep. But I'm willing to meet your terms." He held out a hand. "One escape for one get-out-of-beat-down-free card. What do you say, Marco?"

Marco smiled and took his hand. "Not one. Forever."

Mike tugged on Marco's clasped hand, pulling him closer. "This better work or all bets are off."

Marco jerked his hand out of Mike's death grip. "No deal, then."

"Fine," Mike said. "You show us the escape route and no matter what, hunting season's over."

Was that fear in Mike's voice? Marco couldn't believe it: Richter the Rioter was freaked out. *So there* is *a human being under all that macho crap.* Marco felt like he could trust this human Mike's word. And if they ran into any cops or anything in the service hallways, Marco would have some muscle with him to fend them off. It was too bad he hadn't located Shay first, but opportunity was knocking and this was his best shot.

"Then we have an agreement," he said.

Mike and Drew were ticked when Marco told them that they had to go all the way up to the third floor to get down to the basement. And not only the third floor, but the service corridor by the Grill'n'Shake.

"My card key works for that elevator door and that elevator door only," Marco said. "Otherwise, I could just ride into the service area of the BestBuy and take whatever I wanted from their storage shelves."

"Are you saying that all of these stores have service halls behind them?" Drew asked, brow furrowed like a Neanderthal contemplating his first tool.

"No, this is the only one," Marco said. "The other stores beam in their merchandise."

"How about you check the attitude before he breaks your face." Mike was not amused.

The service corridor was off the public hallway that led to the mall bathrooms. Marco wondered why there weren't more people lined up to use the bathrooms, but as he got closer, the question was answered by his nose. There were outhouses that smelled better.

"Does anyone clean this place?" asked the kid who'd introduced himself as Ryan. He held his hand to his face.

"After cleaning the bathrooms in the Grill'n'Shake,"

Marco said, "I can assure you that trying to keep up with the slobs trapped in this mall would be a full-time job for a four-man cleaning crew."

"So where is this cleaning crew?" Mike said, peeking into the men's room and instantly ducking back out.

"Janitors normally come in at night," Marco said. "Guess no one was here when they locked us in."

"I am so glad we're getting out of here," Drew said.

They arrived at the unmarked service door. Marco checked to make sure no one was watching, then slipped his card key into the scanner and pushed open the door. "This way," he said.

The service corridor was wide—it had to be to roll in the huge pallets of frozen food they used at the Grill'n'Shake and roll out the giant garbage carts. The walls were gray-white, perhaps to match the cement floor, and fluorescent lights hung from the high ceiling. It had all the charm of a morgue.

The elevator required another scan to open it, and yet another to select the floor you wanted to go to. Marco's card opened every one. Once The Three Douches were on board, Marco ran his card and hit PARKING LEVEL, and they began to sink down.

"So what's the plan once we get there?" asked Ryan. He seemed jumpy.

"We pray there are no cops or government agents in hazmat suits and make for the escape hatch." Marco slipped the card back into his pocket.

Everyone stiffened at the idea of meeting anyone official on their little mission. Drew cracked his knuckles like he was cocking his six-shooters for the big showdown.

The elevator dinged and the doors opened on the familiar grayness that was the parking garage service hall. The HVAC fans clicked on and began their growling whir.

"What's that?" Drew asked, sounding like a freaked-out little kid.

"The HVAC fans," Marco said, feeling smugly superior. "Remember? You chased me in there two days ago."

"So that's where you went," Mike said, like he should have known, like it had all been some game of hide-and-seek and not find-and-obliterate.

Marco wanted to say, *That's where I found the bomb that's meant to kill us all,* but decided against it.

Down the hall on the left was the tiny indent in the cement wall with the cheap exit sign over it. Mike peered into the space, suspicious, like Marco was playing some joke, then noticed the hatch in the ceiling. "Well, I'll be a donkey's dick." He whipped a finger at Drew and pointed at the floor. "Down."

Drew complied like the lapdog he was, getting down on all fours. Mike climbed onto his friend's back and began twisting the hatch's wheel-handle. It wound a half turn, then jammed.

"What the," Mike said, throwing all his weight into turning the thing. It wouldn't budge.

"Shrimp," he yelled. "Broom."

Ryan grabbed a broom that had been left leaning against the wall and handed it to Mike. Mike jammed the broom handle into the wheel and tried turning it again. Marco gritted his jaw to mirror Mike's effort. *Turn, you bastard.*

The broom handle snapped.

Mike threw the pieces, dropped off Drew's back, and slammed his fists against the wall. A barbaric grunt accompanied this display. His voice echoed up and down the halls.

Marco felt disappointment seep through his body. If even this exit was locked down, what escape route remained? "Shut up," he said. "Last thing we need is a visit from the cops."

"You shut up, Taco," Mike said. He shoved past Marco and walked toward the service elevator. "Take us back into our prison."

They rode up to the third floor in silence. When they reached the service hall, Mike pushed his way out first, followed by Drew. They stormed down the passage and out into the public hall without so much as a *see you later*. Ryan, however, clapped a hand on Marco's shoulder before leaving the elevator.

"Thanks," he said.

"For nothing," Marco added.

Ryan shrugged. "At least we tried." He ran down the hall after his fellow Douches.

Marco checked his watch. He'd wasted an hour. Seveglia would be looking for him. Marco decided to abandon his search for the senator's kid and Shay. There was no sense in pissing off the boss by being late. He would already have to explain away Roberto's abduction. He took the service corridor to the back entrance of the Grill'n'Shake and prepared for his fifth shift.

L
E
X
I

Knowing one's way around a home electronics department had its advantages. When Lexi noticed that the police communicated with the medical teams through walkie-talkies, she picked up a multi-frequency scanner at the HomeMart and took the liberty of modifying it to listen in on their conversation. No need to snoop on the PaperClips now that she had one of these babies. She slid on some headphones and leaned back on her unicorn comforter to let the information come to her.

At first the chatter was bland. Then it got interesting.

"Samples have been prepped for testing."

Then it got terrifying.

"Negative for smallpox. Beginning tests for tularemia. Team considering not going forward with Ebola screen as too few dead."

She dropped the thing onto the tile.

"You okay, hon?" her dad called. He was trying to organize something for the Senator at a computer across the room.

Lexi snatched back the scanner, pressed it against her chest.

"Yes," she yelled, too loud.

She scrambled onto the stool, hacked the Internet, and began searching for what the hell tularemia was.

The Internet was surprisingly helpful. She found all sorts of information on bioterrorism. Signs and symptoms of various toxins. After scanning a few webpages, she needed to excuse herself to the bathroom to throw up.

So this was what the evil scientists were looking for.

Deadly bioweapons.

She had to walk. Every time someone coughed, she lurched the other way. The flimsy surgical masks she could get at the pharmacy wouldn't protect her, so she focused on what she could do: hand washing, avoiding physical contact with other human beings. From her vomit-visit, she knew the bathrooms were the last place one should go to wash one's hands, so she bought a giant bottle of hand sanitizer. She'd rubbed the stuff over her skin about fifty times.

The portable scanner dragged down the pockets of Lexi's hoodie, knocking against her thighs as she walked back toward the Apple Store.

"Hey, baby," some kid across the hall howled. "Nice humps." Then he started singing that song. Badly. "In the back and in the front, you got them workin'."

"Jerk off," she mumbled, and walked faster.

Back in the Apple Store, she tried to work on her movie. She had to do something other than rub alcohol on her hands. But every few minutes, a question would pop into her brain, like *Did he say* dead*? Have people* DIED*???*

The Senator pushed open the stockroom doors just before seven. She'd been going back and forth to the PaperClips using some maze of back hallways.

"I need to talk with you," Lexi growled from the shadows.

Her mother started, eyes widening in shock, then sighed. "Really, Lex," she said, rubbing her forehead, "I'm about ready to keel over as it is."

"I saw the PaperClips." Lexi slid the scanner across the desktop. "And I heard what they're testing people for."

Two cops shuffled into the stockroom behind the Senator and she waved them into the store. The stockroom doors closed, leaving Lexi and the Senator alone in the dim light shining from between the shelves.

The Senator considered Lexi for a moment, then sank into the chair at the desk. "You sure you want to know?"

Gooseflesh pricked out along Lexi's skin. She hadn't expected the Senator to give in so easily.

"Yes," she said, feigning certainty. "Are you really going to tell me?"

The Senator smirked. "I know you think I still see you as my little baby, but I know you're a big girl now."

Her use of the phrase "big girl" nearly put Lexi through the roof.

Dotty wrapped her fingers around Lexi's hand. "You're sticky," she said.

"Hand sanitizer," Lexi said.

Dotty squeezed her fingers. "Good thinking." She explained that a small device of unknown origin was discovered in the parking garage by some kid. The thing was attached to the ventilation system for a part of the mall. It pumped something into the air.

"A biotoxin?" Lexi asked, her voice cracking on the word.

"That's what we're trying to figure out in the medical ward," Dotty said, as if a biotoxin were merely an air freshener. "We're testing people to see if anything's wrong with them. The device itself kind of imploded when the Feds pried it off the air duct—we couldn't get a reading of what had been inside it."

"Have people died?"

Dotty exhaled slowly. "As far as I know, one old woman, but that could be unrelated."

"So what are they going to do once they figure out what's in the air?" Lexi's leg began to jiggle.

"Then the medical teams will start working to fix it. Federal agents are handling most of the operations now, so my information is limited to what they decide I need to know. I'm hoping the tests say it's plague." She crossed her fingers and looked to the heavens. "Come on, plague!"

Lexi laughed. It wasn't funny, but she desperately needed to laugh. "When plague's your best-case scenario, you know you're in trouble."

"At least plague is curable."

Dotty dropped her hand back onto Lexi's. They sat there, hand in hand, for a moment. Then Lexi slid down off the desk. "Thanks for telling me," she said.

"I trust you," her mother said.

"Does Dad know?"

"He does." Dotty stood and pulled her jacket straight. "But we need to keep this between the three of us, okay?"

"You're not going to tell people?"

"Not until we know what we're dealing with," she said, sounding more like the Senator. "We don't want people to panic."

"Who's the we?" Lexi asked, stepping back.

Dotty gave her a playful punch on the arm. "The good guys," she said. "Your friendly local government and FEMA overlords."

"Why does that not make me feel better?"

"We try our very best to not make everything worse," Dotty said. "Old government motto." She smiled at Lexi. "So are we in agreement? We keep this a Ross family secret?"

"Like all those gold-plated toilet seats we keep in the basement?"

"Exactly," Dotty said, putting an arm around Lexi.

Lexi didn't even try to shrug it off.

They decided to go to Chopsticky Buns for dinner. It turned out to be the best meal the family had shared in a long while. Mom and Dad joked about lapses in personal hygiene. Lexi didn't feel the need to make any snarky comments. She was steeped in a soup of warm fuzzies for her parents. *And all it took was one life-threatening bomb.*

There were only two smudges on the otherwise perfect evening: One, Dotty was tailed by two security guards (*a little over the top, no?*); and two, Chopsticky Buns had run out of egg rolls. Dotty seemed unduly disappointed about the latter.

"We'll get you one after dinner from the food court," Lexi said, seeing her mother's face droop at the news.

Dotty flashed a small smile. "Yeah," she said. She picked up her phone and began tapping out a text.

After dinner, they began their trek back down to the Apple Store. Just as they stepped off the escalator onto the first floor, a woman came up to Dotty.

"Excuse me," she said. "You're the Senator, right?"

The woman didn't look good. She had bags under her eyes and her clothes smelled like a locker room. A man stood a few feet behind her with two small kids. One of the kids had a runny nose that was dripping off her upper lip.

Dotty shifted her body so that Lexi was behind her. "Yes," she said. "Can I help you?"

"I heard you were in charge of this nightmare," the woman said, not even trying to control the tone of her voice. "And I need you to let us out of here." She pointed at the man and two kids. "My kids can't sleep on those cots in the hallway, and we're all at our wits' end."

Dotty straightened herself and put on her "official" voice, the one she used for the mall announcements. "I'm sorry, ma'am. We're working as quickly as possible to resolve the situation—"

"Don't give me that double-talk nonsense!" the woman shouted. Lexi noticed other shoppers had begun to stare.

One of the guards approached the woman. "Please step back, ma'am."

The woman looked at him like she was just itching to slug him in the jaw. "Don't you touch me," she said. "I want to know why this woman is holding us in here, that's all."

This did not seem like the ideal moment to tell the woman that the best-case scenario was an outbreak of the plague.

The guard puffed out his chest. "I'm going to ask you again, ma'am. Please *step back*."

The woman's husband came to her side. "We know our rights," the man said. "We just want to get out of here."

Another man approached. "Yeah, let us out of here." He turned to the other people who'd gathered in their stretch of hallway, pumped his fist in the air, and began to chant. "Let us out! Let us out!" Others joined in. Lexi saw the guard pull a walkie-talkie from his belt and mumble something into it.

Arthur came up behind Lexi and grabbed her shoulders. "Come with me now," he whispered in her ear. He tugged her away from Dotty.

"What about Mom?" Lexi said, stumbling away from her.

"She'd want to be sure you were safe," Arthur said. They began to run back to the Apple Store. As they ran, the chanting got louder.

It was like watching a storm roll in. From the front window of the Apple Store, Lexi could see where they'd left her mother standing in the hallway. Lexi pressed herself against the floor-to-ceiling glass and watched, horrified, as more and more people crowded together. Their shouts echoed around the open spaces of the mall like thunder.

Lexi pulled out her phone. She needed to talk to Darren. She opened a text, then saw that there was no signal. Not that she couldn't get through—there was no cell signal at

all. *Our friendly FEMA overlords must be using a damper.*
This explained the near-constant congestion of the cell
signal; now they'd simply jammed the entire frequency.
The government did not want the riot tweeted.

A troop of twenty mall security guys bearing full-body
plastic shields marched into the hallway. They banged on
the back of the shields with police batons. One held a
megaphone and repeated over and over, "Remain calm!
Step back against the walls!" No one seemed to be listening. The crowd's chanting grew louder. The people turned
from her mother to face the oncoming invasion.

Something hit the glass above Lexi with a bang. She
fell back on her hands, breathless, and glanced up. A
spiderweb of fractures surrounded a white puncture. On
the ground were the remains of a cell phone. If she were
four inches taller, it would have nailed her between the
eyes.

Ginger and Maddie staggered into the Apple Store,
screaming.

"What is going on?" Maddie yelled to no one in particular.

Ginger slumped against a counter. "I just wanted my
comforter," she mumbled. "I didn't want to sleep on the
floor again."

No hello. No glad to see you. They'd been shopping.
Both wore new clothes: Ginger, a fluffy pink sweater, and
Maddie, a see-through tee with a black bra.

Lexi stood and wiped the dust from her jeans. "Then
take it and leave before things get any worse."

Maddie gawked at her. "You want us to leave?"

A bottle flew through the open entry and smashed against the table. Ginger screamed as shards of green glass exploded into her side.

Lexi rushed to her. "We have to get away from this door," she said, thrusting a shoulder under Ginger's arm.

Maddie nodded and pushed Ginger off the table, who stumbled, sobbing, after Lexi.

One of the Senator's police detail burst into the Apple Store with one arm around Dotty's shoulder. He pointed to the Apple salespeople. "You have a security gate?" he asked.

A woman nodded and held up a key.

"Close it!" he shouted. He dropped Dotty next to a table and ran out.

Lexi lowered Ginger onto her comforter.

Maddie mumbled a string of profanity under her breath, eyes teary with concern.

Lexi pulled a large shard from Ginger's arm. There was no blood.

"I think the sweater took most of the damage," Lexi said, smiling.

Maddie shoved Ginger, then started crying. "Don't freaking do that to me!"

Ginger laughed through her tears. "I guess I tend to overreact when assaulted by glassware."

They pulled the largest pieces from Ginger's sweater, then she carefully pulled the thing off. She had a few superficial scrapes, but nothing serious.

"This tank is so unflattering," Ginger said, pulling at the fabric of her undershirt.

"Lucky for you," Lexi said, "the last thing anyone is looking at right now is your shirt."

The Senator was busy organizing the fear-stricken Apple staff. They'd closed the security gates and now rushed about boxing up any exposed computer equipment.

"Let's get away from the madness," Lexi said, and led Maddie and Ginger into the stockroom. As they slammed the door shut behind them, they heard the telltale crash of a shattering storefront window.

"What is wrong with people?" Maddie said, slumping into the seat at the desk where only a few hours ago Lexi had interrogated her mother.

She could tell them, explain everything. They'd be grateful. Maybe grateful enough to be her friend.

She didn't need friends that badly.

"They've been locked in a mall for three days," Lexi said.

"I guess the Muzak's enough to drive even the sanest person nuts," Maddie said.

"Maybe they really wanted to go to work," Ginger said.

Maddie looked at her like she'd grown a harelip. "Yeah, they're rioting so they can get back to the office."

"I missed ballet class," Ginger said. "No way I'm getting Coppelia in the winter recital now."

Maddie kicked her feet onto the desk. "Well, I got out of field hockey practice. Thank you, security situation."

Lexi wondered what she'd missed. She was a member of no club, no sport. She'd checked in on her online worlds—nothing missed there.

"I had a bio lab," Lexi added. It was all she could think of.

Neither reacted. They probably sensed she had no outside life to lose.

"I'm bored," Maddie said. "Maybe we should go back out to the riot."

Ginger shoved Maddie's feet off the desk and sat down. "I'm not risking my life to give you a thrill."

"What about that time I convinced you to go skydiving?"

Ginger rolled her eyes. "We had parachutes."

All these things to do in the real world. Lexi had watched some YouTube videos about skydiving to get ideas for CG camera moves.

"We could listen to it," Lexi offered, pulling the scanner from her pocket. She flicked the machine on. After a squeal and a crackle, they heard hysterical shouting, screams, muffled blows.

"Launch the tear gas!" a voice shouted.

"Not in a confined space!" *The Senator.*

A muffled boom like a gunshot. More screams.

Lexi slid the scanner onto the desktop and they huddled around it, silent, mesmerized. After some time, they noticed that they were holding on to one another. And when the screams finally died down, when the chatter over the scanner became mere orders to herd the former rioters into their stores, the three stayed there, woven together, until Lights Out buried them in darkness and they curled on the cement floor to sleep.

DAY

FOUR

· TUESDAY ·

SHAY

There were limits to how long a person could remain positive in the face of adversity, and Shay had reached hers. She had spent the night in SnoozeSelect taking care of Nani, who shivered with cold one minute and threw her blankets off the next. Around midnight, she developed a cough. Of course, when Shay asked Nani what was wrong, she said *It's nothing, I'm feeling better, just a cold.* How was Shay supposed to help when Nani lied about her symptoms?

Although the mall god had announced at Lights On that free food would be provided at the former testing stations, there was a long line at the Burger Baron. Shay had eaten her free ration, but was hoping the servers would give her some soup, as Nani refused to eat solid food.

Shay had scoured the entire diabetes section of the *Merck Manual,* for which she'd paid a significant chunk of change yesterday afternoon, and had found nothing to explain what a cough and chills had to do with diabetes. She'd ordered Preeti to buy Tylenol, since that was what Ba gave them when they were sick, but Nani couldn't swallow the pills. She spat them out, complaining that the pills stuck in her throat. So Shay had Preeti get children's liquid Tylenol. Nani spilled half the bottle when a fit of coughing took her mid-sip.

Apart from the two shopping trips, Preeti had been useless. She whined about going to Hollister, how Shay had *promised* they could sleep in Hollister. Shay had finally blown up at her and screamed *You want to go to Hollister, then go!* And Preeti had left.

"We're out of toaster sticks," the girl at the register droned when Shay reached the front of the line.

"Do you have any soup?"

The girl spoke into her headset mic. Shay heard the voice on the other end reply in the negative. "Not until noon," she said.

"Then just a coffee," Shay said, dropping a bill on the counter.

Shay slunk away from the registers with her steaming cup and plopped into a seat. She considered going to the clothing depot—along with the free food, it had been announced that people on the outside had donated clothing—but from the shouts echoing up from the first-floor fountain, it sounded like it was already too much of a madhouse. She was definitely not volunteering for the requested "Cleanup Crew." No gift certificate was worth entering the bathrooms for longer than absolutely necessary.

Brilliant sunlight streamed through the glass ceiling. Shay closed her eyes, let the bright light burn through her eyelids. It must have been a beautiful day outside. She tried to remember what day it even was.

"Hey there."

Shay cracked open her eyes and shielded them with her hand. Ryan stood in front of her, the sunlight behind him forming a blazing halo. God, he was pretty.

"I'm so glad I found you," he said. He had a bruise on his face. Somehow, it made him even better looking.

"You were looking for me?" she asked, trying to seem nonchalant.

He smiled that irresistible half smile. "Well, yeah," he said. "We have a date to make up."

His use of the word *date* energized her better than any cup of coffee. Preeti was in Hollister, Nani was fast asleep . . .

"You want to go to the bookstore?" she asked, standing. Was she trembling from lack of sleep or the nearness of him? She rolled and unrolled the hem of her kameez between her fingers.

"Can we go somewhere else first?" he asked. "I want to show you something. It's kind of my secret."

"We're already sharing secrets?" she asked.

"I read your poems."

"Tagore's poems," she corrected. "What secrets of mine could you learn reading them?"

"You made notes in the margins," he said. "Your favorite poem"—he sat and began folding a napkin—"is about a flower"—he took her coffee stirrer—"only the spirit can touch." He lifted his creation: a paper flower on a stirrer stem. He held it out to her. "My mom taught me to make these."

He took her hand, gently, his fingers slowly winding into hers, and pressed the flower to her palm. Warmth radiated from Shay's hand to her body, out, then down.

"Onward?" she asked.

"Onward," he answered.

Ryan handed Shay a mess of nylon webbing. "You have to, um," he stammered, "put this around your, well, legs?" He was blushing. "Here, let me show you."

He stepped into the two bottom loops, then pulled the waistband, sliding the loops up his jeans, and fastened the harness like a belt. "See?" He lifted his shirt slightly, exposing smooth skin and just the barest hint of navel, then pointed, like she wasn't already staring. She wondered if he was really just showing her the harness.

Two can play this game.

"I think my kameez is going to get in the way," she said. "I'll be right back."

She walked—feet barely touching the tiles—to a changing room, undid her choli, and slipped the kameez over her head. She then pulled the choli back on, fastened the clasps between her shoulder blades, and slipped the harness over her jeans.

The choli fit tightly around her curves, ending just above her waist, leaving her belly exposed to the top of her low-riding jeans. The harness wrapped around her natural waist, the padding hugged her skin. She liked her body. Why not show it?

Stepping out of the room, she saw that her plan had the desired effect. Ryan's jaw unhinged itself, he looked so stunned. *Maybe he really was just showing me the harness . . . ?*

She swallowed the nervousness that bubbled inside at this realization and decided to just play it cool. So she'd upped the ante. He was a boy for whom the ante should be upped.

"Now what?" she said as if she were confident in her half nakedness.

"Huh?" he said. "Uh, ropes." He snatched a rope from the wall. It was already knotted around a metal D-ring. "You want to go first?" he asked. He seemed to be fighting the urge to drop his gaze.

"Sure," she said.

He paused for a moment, then reached forward and quickly slipped the ring around a small loop on the front of her harness. His hands came distressingly close to her skin. Gooseflesh pimpled her belly.

He stepped back, his cheeks fiery with blush, and attached a different metal gizmo to his harness. "Now climb," he said. "I've got you." He looked into her eyes and flashed his half smile, and she knew that he did.

Standing nose-to-wall, she wrapped her hands around two small lumpy handholds just above her head, put one foot on another lump, then lifted off the ground. As she moved spider-like up the wall, she felt him tighten the rope between them.

"You're almost there," he shouted.

She reached up and touched the ceiling. There was a small ledge nearby and she scooted herself onto it. She wasn't high off the ground, but she may as well have been orbiting the earth, from the dizzy feeling she got looking back down at him.

"Now jump!" he said. He pulled the slack from her rope.

She leaned back off the ledge, feeling the strength of his hold on her, then dropped, her hair whipping across her face, until the rope caught her, jolting her, forcing a yelp of laughter from her already smiling lips.

He lowered her down slowly. She hung limp until she felt her feet touch the ground.

"Great, right?" he said, steadying her.

"Amazing."

He climbed next. He moved expertly up the wall, his hands gripping holds barely bigger than a knuckle. When he reached the top, he sat on the ledge and switched the D-ring to the back of his harness.

"You got me?" he said.

She tugged the rope tighter. "I've got you."

And he fell, his eyes locked on hers as he swept toward her. She nearly let go of the rope, she was so overwhelmed by him. But she held on, catching his weight against her hips. He smiled, feeling the sudden link between them, and kept smiling all the way down.

"I can't believe that was your first time," he said. "Climbing, I mean." The rope hung limp between them.

"I had a good teacher." Shay felt an incredible urge to touch him, but feared she might burst into flame.

A sales guy came over to reprimand Ryan for using the back loop on the harness, blathering on about liability or something, but they just detached themselves from the rope, slipped out of their harnesses, grabbed her bag, and drifted away from him.

When they reached the door, Ryan took her hand and the sensation sent shock waves across her skin.

"What next?" she asked.

But really, who cared? So long as they were together.

LEXI

O h my god," Maddie squealed, sloshing her decaf
mocha inside its paper cup, "you have to tell her
about Tomo's party the other weekend!"

It was like the riot had never happened; the mess had
been cleaned by the Feds overnight and even the fear was
hard to recall, sitting now as Lexi was in the food court,
the place where "everyone" hung out, according to Maddie. Lexi noticed that the halls for the most part were
devoid of grown-ups. Maybe they'd been scared into
hiding. But not the teens.

Ginger was mid-sip and began shaking with laughter.
"Sorry," she mumbled, trying to swallow without snarfing
her latte. "Too funny."

"Fine," Maddie said. "I'll tell her."

Maddie began regaling Lexi with another tale from the
History of Irvington Country Day. Apparently, it was not

all tea parties and polo games. The last story ended with, "And then we had to call the fire department because the bonfire lit up the grass clippings in the lawn."

So this was the life she'd been denied by sticking with video games and computer programming. She'd never seen an entire lawn ablaze before. Maybe everything was more fun when there was a bit of terror lurking in the shadows. Take, for instance, Maddie Flynn. Not the brightest chip on the circuit board, but totally entertaining. Her stories helped distract Lexi from the fact that one floor below, down a short hall, government scientists were figuring out whether or not she had Ebola. (Probably not—she had yet to start bleeding out her eyes.)

Maddie was up on a chair now, imitating the dance some girl had done across the diving board of Tomo's pool. "And then she totally fell in, drink and all!" Maddie stepped down off the seat.

"Why'd you stop the show?" some asshole hollered from across the food court.

"In your dreams, dickweed," Maddie screamed back, not even looking.

"How do you put up with it?" Lexi asked.

"Boys are stupid," Maddie said, swilling more coffee. "They're always thinking with their crotch."

"I wish my boobs were worthy of a shout-out," Ginger said. "But I'd rather have ballet than boobs."

"I hate it," Lexi said.

"So a guy likes your tits and says so. Why let it get to you?" Maddie asked, giving Lexi the raised-eyebrow once-over.

"I'm not like you," Lexi said. Maddie's eyebrows sunk into a scowl. Lexi scrambled for a better explanation. "I mean, I'm not good with boys."

Now their interest was piqued.

"Have you ever been kissed?" Ginger asked.

"No."

Maddie leaned over the table, a wicked smile unfurling across her face. "I dare you to go up to"—she flicked a purple-painted nail—"that table, and offer one of those guys a lap dance."

Lexi glanced over. The guys at the table were normal-looking. Not her normal guys, but normal-looking by everyone else's standards: rumpled, chiseled, shaggy-haired. It was only a dance.

"What do I get if I do it?" Lexi asked. An airy feeling expanded through her stomach, sent tingles to her fingers.

"You get to dare me to do something," Maddie said.

What a proposition: A measly dance for control over Maddie Flynn? *Done and done.* "Fine," Lexi said.

She stood up. She'd seen movies. She knew what to do. What boys were looking for. So she had never really "danced" before (she and Darren spent middle school dances at home playing Halo online). It couldn't be that hard. She didn't have to touch the guy, and he couldn't touch her—there were rules. *Right?*

She was in front of them.

"What?" one of the guys grunted.

Lexi gulped down what felt like an ocean of saliva. "Wh-which one of you would like a lap dance?"

The boys looked at one another, then burst out laughing. Lexi remained calm. She popped her hip out, giving them a full view of her generous rump. Then she unzipped her hoodie. She was wearing a normal T-shirt, but with her boobs, normal T-shirts were revealing. She pulled the ends of each sleeve and then shimmied (awkwardly) the sweatshirt the rest of the way off.

Now she had their attention. One took the bait. "Okay," he said. "I mean, why not?"

Lexi glanced over at Maddie and Ginger. They were leaning over the tabletop. Maddie's hand shooed her on.

Lexi strutted forward, one hand on hip. She slowly walked around the guy's chair, swishing her ass back and forth, taking it slow to give her more time to think up what to do next. When she reached the front of his chair, she bent forward, shoving her butt in his face.

"Yeah, back up that junk," one of the guys said.

And at that very moment, she farted.

If she could have deleted herself from the universe, she would have.

Blood pulsed in her ears. She could die of shame or she could own that fart.

She stood straight up and spun around. "That's what you get for calling my body junk," she said.

"Oh, foul!" the boys said, waving their hands in front of their faces. "Dude, you got played!"

Lexi picked up her hoodie, swung it jauntily over her shoulder, and sashayed back to the gaping Maddie and Ginger.

"Holy crap!" Maddie said, laughing.

"That was totally gross!" Ginger said, eyes wide with awe.

Maddie flopped back into her chair. "Did you really do that on purpose?" she asked.

A billion butterflies batted their wings against Lexi's belly. She was light-headed.

"Hell yeah, I did." Lexi said. There were moments in which one should tell the truth. This was not one of them. She was cool. She was in control. She turned to Maddie. "Now it's my turn. I dare you to do that dance again on the chair."

"*La*-ame," Maddie sang.

Lexi dug into her brain—to what depths did one have to sink to impress someone like Maddie?

"Fine," she said. "I dare you to streak the ice-skating rink."

Maddie's eyes sparkled. "You are on."

They'd been at it all day, and Lexi was exhausted. Maddie had gotten a rash from falling butt-naked onto the ice, Ginger was wanted by the saleslady at Sephora for stealing lipsticks, and Lexi had slid on her stomach all the way down a bowling lane, knocking over the pins with her head (seven-ten split), and was now banned from playing there for life. They'd been at it all day, and Lexi was exhilarated.

After a dinner spent recounting the day's insanity, they'd retired to Abercrombie, where the other resident teens had begun to gather.

Lexi turned to Maddie. "Truth: How many of these guys have you kissed?"

Maddie waved her hand around. "Truth sucks. Give me a dare."

"Truth or dare," a male voice cooed. "My kind of game."

Three boys materialized out of the pheromone-laced shadows.

"Welcome to the naughty circle," Maddie said, patting the floor beside her and batting her bedroom eyes.

The boys inserted themselves between Lexi and Maddie. One eyed Lexi's chest, then looked her in the eye and gave her a chin jut of approval. Lexi's skin crawled.

"I dare you," Maddie said, pointing at one of the boys, "to take off your shirt."

The guy smiled, checked in with his bros on either side, then lifted his tee, revealing abs the likes of which Lexi had only glimpsed on a screen.

More kids appeared. There was nothing like a sex game to lure in the masses.

"Me next," a newcomer said. "I dare you"—he pointed to a blond girl in a tank—"to take off your clothes."

She giggled, then began peeling off her top.

The room felt too dark. The racks of clothes pressed in on Lexi.

"Now me," said the underwear-clad girl. "I dare you to kiss her." She pointed at a brunette in a sweater who blushed, but leaned forward, eager.

Lexi did not want her first kiss to be the result of a dare. Some sloppy, slimy, droolfest across the wood floor of an Abercrombie.

The two kissed. Somewhere in the shadows, a kid coughed. The word *Ebola* flashed in neon behind Lexi's eyes.

This was dangerous. There were germs, people. The two kissers separated. The girl licked her lips. The boy sneezed.

This game was like freaking Russian roulette.

Maddie was on the other side of the circle, but Ginger was still next to Lexi. She seemed to be intently watching the game, leaning forward after each dare like she was hoping some guy would notice her.

"We have to get out of here," Lexi whispered into Ginger's ear.

"Huh?" Ginger glanced at her. "Don't worry," she said. "If you don't want to do it, just say 'Pass.' "

"It's not that," Lexi said. "I mean, it is that, but it's something more."

Ginger looked at her. "Okay, what?"

From across the circle: "I dare those two to kiss." He was pointing at Lexi and Ginger.

Ginger blanched.

Lexi grabbed Ginger's arm, dragging her to her feet. "We pass." She pulled Ginger into a pool of shadow. Hoots of disappointment burst from the circle.

"What are you doing?" Ginger said, wrenching her arm from Lexi's grasp.

"Saving your life." Lexi was trying to be vague. She wouldn't be divulging any secrets so long as she was vague.

"What are you talking about?" Ginger asked. She was getting mad now. She glanced at the circle. Another couple was kissing.

"The security situation," Lexi said. She instantly had Ginger's attention.

"Did your mom tell you something?"

How to say as little as possible . . .

"The medical teams," Lexi blurted. "They think there's

something in the air, like we're infected with something."

Ginger's eyes teared up. "Are we going to die?"

"No," Lexi said, covering. "No, it's just that you could get sick. I mean, they have cures for the stuff, but you don't want to go through that."

"Oh my god," she said. She looked at the circle. "We should tell them, stop them."

Lexi grabbed her arm before she could move. "No!" She scrambled for a reason. "No, I mean, my mom said that they were just going to cure everyone without saying anything, to avoid freaking people out. That—that's actually what the testing is. But you still don't want to get the illness. We should go." Lexi began walking toward the exit.

Ginger followed. "I need to call my dad."

"They shut down the phones and the Internet."

"But your scanner," Ginger said, pleading. "It's like those things truckers have, right?"

"Your dad's a lawyer, not a trucker." They were in the well-lit hall now. Lexi's breathing slowed. She felt calmer. *Why didn't I think of using a CB before?*

"But maybe we can reach a trucker, maybe they can call my dad." Ginger grabbed her arm, pulled Lexi around to face her. "I need to talk to him."

The girl was white as death. All Lexi had wanted was to get out of the store. She owed Ginger something. And didn't Ginger's dad deserve to know at least that Ginger was all right?

"I have a friend, Darren," Lexi said. "He used to have a CB radio, built it from one of those kits. Maybe I can reach him, and he can call your dad."

Ginger threw her arms around Lexi. "Thank you," she

said, then she pulled away, blushing. "Sorry," she said. "I guess we shouldn't hug anymore."

"No," Lexi said. An oil slick of regret began to bubble in her gut.

Lexi bought a portable CB radio (Dad was going to blow a transistor when he got his credit card bill) and led Ginger to a quiet corner in the home section of the JCPenney (far from the Senator's prying ears). They took some fake LED candles from a Halloween display to light the way. It wasn't Lights Out yet, but the staff had switched off half the lights. Someone snored nearby.

Nestled in a pile of throw pillows, Lexi clicked to the channel she and Darren had used as kids. "DMaster?" she whispered into the mic. "You out there?"

"This feels like a séance," Ginger said, slinking closer to Lexi.

"Darren?" she said again.

"Lexi?" He was there. He was waiting for her.

She felt a tear trickle down her cheek. "It's me," she said, smiling just to hear his voice.

"I left the radio on, in case you remembered. What's going on in there?" he asked. "The news people are talking dirty bombs."

"It's not a dirty bomb," Lexi said. Then instantly regretted it.

"Wait, you know what's going on?"

Why didn't he ask if she was okay? Shouldn't that have been his first question?

"Look, everything's going to be fine," she said. "I need you to do me a favor."

"Yeah, sure," he said. "So what's it like in there? Are people going crazy?"

For all their years of friendship, did he even know her? Did he even care?

"It's totally normal," Lexi said. "Like any other day at the mall." She let go of the TALK button.

"Why are you lying to him?" Ginger said. "I thought he was your best friend."

The CB crackled. "That sucks," he said. "These past couple days, I had kinda wished I'd gone to the mall with you. It sounded like it might have been cool."

"Being trapped in the CommerceDome is suddenly cool?" Lexi asked.

"At least it would be different."

A trapdoor snapped open in Lexi's brain, releasing the understanding that boredom had been the bedrock of her former life. Funny how she'd never seen the games and movies for what they were: ways of passing time while in a holding pattern, waiting for real life to begin. *Is this real life?* If so, she preferred boredom.

"Ask him about my dad," Ginger said, reminding Lexi of why they'd bothered contacting Darren.

Lexi clicked the TALK button. "I need you to call someone for me and say exactly what I tell you to, okay?"

"Can't he go and get my dad?" Ginger said, tears beginning to form in her eyes. "Can't I talk to him myself?"

"Would your dad really follow some random kid he doesn't know home to use his CB?"

Ginger wilted. "I guess not."

The CB squeaked. "Who am I calling?" Darren asked.

"My friend wants to talk to her dad," Lexi answered.

Ginger said the number.

"It's ringing," Darren said.

When the line picked up, Ginger began dictating to Darren. There were several minutes of back and forth establishing that this call was for real, and then Ginger sobbed to her parents about how she was fine and that they all couldn't be trapped in here for much longer because the government people were curing everyone.

"Curing everyone?" Darren said.

"Yeah," Ginger said. "Tell my dad the security situation is some disease, but they're curing it and then we can all go free."

The icy fingers of the oil slick strangled Lexi from within.

"How do they know there's a cure?" Darren asked.

"Is that my dad asking or you?"

"Both."

"Lexi said."

Silence.

"He's not buying it," Darren said.

Lexi grabbed the CB from Ginger. "Make him buy it," she said. She felt light-headed, her heart was racing.

"He hung up," Darren said.

"Call him back!" Ginger wailed.

Silence. "The line's busy," Darren said.

Ginger flung herself into the pillows and sobbed.

The mall speakers announced Lights Out and they were shrouded in darkness. The fake candles flickered, throwing huge shadows against the shelves.

"You still there?" Darren asked.

"Where else am I going to go?" Lexi said.

"So you're really okay in there?"

At least he thought to ask. "Yeah, I'm fine. Everything's fine."

Silence. Ginger sobbing.

"Well, I was in the middle of a game."

"Oh." Darkness. Someone snuffling in another aisle. "What game?"

"Just some Halo."

"The regular guys?"

"Some new kids. I'm sniping the crap out of them. They have no idea what they're doing."

"Sounds boring."

"Nothing else to do."

Lexi felt a sob catch in her throat. "Well, I'd hate for you to let those noobs off the hook because of me."

"Like I'd ever. Radio me again?"

"Yeah," Lexi said, knowing she would not.

"Hang tough, my sister," he said.

"Yeah. Hang tough."

She turned the CB off and fell back into the pillows. She stared at the flickering shadows until her tears blurred them into nothing.

M
A
R
C
O

Marco staked out the Apple Store all morning
watching for the girl in the hoodie, aka the senator's daughter. Shards of glass were embedded
in the carpet outside the store; spilled dirt darkened the
fibers in the rug near one of the large potted plants and
the tree in it stood at an odd angle. Still, someone had
done a good job cleaning the worst of it up. You could
almost pretend there'd been no riot here last night.

The girl in the hoodie never showed, so there was nothing to do but retreat to the restaurant. On his way back,
Marco noticed other changes brought on by the riot. There
were now guys in hazmat suits roaming the halls with riot
shields and long poles that looked like cattle prods. He
was not sure this was the wisest decision.

As if reading his mind, a group of kids jumped on a
hazmat cop from behind. The cop began whacking at them
with the shield and cattle prod. Then a kid got the prod

away from him. Two other hazmat cops appeared and Tasered the kids, dropping them onto the tiles. One cop retrieved the pilfered Taser from the boy's limp hand.

Marco wasn't the only one watching. Some adults cheered. A few carried mops or wore gloves—evidence that at least some people had volunteered for the government's Cleanup Crew. A group of kids whispered conspiratorially.

Marco guessed that it would take twenty-four hours, maybe less, for the government to realize that the hazmat cops just provided the assholes with a target for all their pent-up rage. By tomorrow, the asylum would once again belong to the inmates.

To avoid running into any more mini-riots, Marco took the service elevator up to the Grill'n'Shake. Josh was manning the host station when Marco emerged from the back, wrapping his apron around his waist.

"It's ten to twelve, Ensign Cohen. Lunch rush, ahoy."

Josh continued to roll silverware. "You want to get the Enforcer or do I have to?"

The Enforcer was how they'd come to refer to Mr. Seveglia. He'd taken over running the bar after the bartender, a college girl named Heather, started coughing into the drinks. Once relieved of duty, Heather had taken off. No one had seen her since.

"I've got it," Marco said, returning into the maze of the dining room.

Mr. Seveglia looked worse than he had this morning— Marco hadn't thought the man could look any more ticked-off than he had when they made the announcement about the free food giveaway. "It wasn't bad enough they locked us in here," he'd said, "but they take away our ability to do business as well?" Now he looked kind of sick and crazy in addition to ticked. The glare from the computer screen gave his skin the pallor of moldy bread.

The Enforcer didn't look up from his screen. "We've run out of Onion Explosions," he said. "Wings will be next."

Marco wasn't sure what the man was getting at. "That's terrible, sir," he said.

"Terrible is only the beginning of it, son," he said. "The free food is apparently disgusting enough that we still have customers, but they'll feel a financial crunch soon enough and then they'll eat what the Feds give 'em."

"No way," Marco said. "People have credit cards."

Mr. Seveglia tapped the screen. "We'll run out of food in two days anyway. Then what, my boy?" The Enforcer ducked his head and coughed violently, then pulled out a tissue and blew his nose.

Was the suggestion here that Mr. Seveglia was planning on closing up shop? Marco would not let that happen. Could not.

"The halls are not safe," he began. "I've been sneaking out there, trying to learn what I can about this security situation."

"Oh yeah?" Mr. Seveglia said, then gulped down what looked like tea.

"People need a place to eat. The government might be handing out food, but they're not handing out tables, and the food court's run by gangs at this point. Why not let people use the restaurant? It could be a safe haven for families. And maybe they'd still buy drinks."

Mr. Seveglia coughed again. "I like this thinking," he said. "What else you got?"

Marco groped around in his brain. "The bathrooms!" he said, the gears really beginning to spin. "The crews the government tried to pull together to clean the main johns have done shoddy work at best. If we keep ours clean, we can charge people—"

"A buck?" Mr. Seveglia was looking livelier by the second.

"Too much," Marco said. "It has to be a token, something people won't care too much about. A quarter."

"Like they're feeding—*cough*—the meter."

"Exactly."

Mr. Seveglia stood, clapped Marco on the shoulder. Marco wished the man wouldn't touch him; the Enforcer had just used that hand to wipe his running nose. Marco couldn't afford to get the cold that was going around.

"We'll stay in business yet," Mr. Seveglia said, gulping down the last of his liquid. "Time for lunch, eh?"

Mr. Seveglia steered Marco out of the office, locked it behind them. As they walked toward the front, Marco saw Shay standing near the host station.

She was okay.

She had come back to him.

To thank him for helping her get insulin for her grandmother? She should have known no thanks were necessary. But it was a nice gesture. Marco paused to look in one of the tchotchke mirrors that adorned the walls of the Grill'n'Shake. His hair wasn't terrible. His face—well, what could you do?

He turned, ready to welcome her, sit her down, maybe join her for a quick lunch before things really got going at the restaurant, and saw that she was not alone. She was here with that douche Ryan. From the way she leaned toward him, Marco knew that they were more than friends.

She was not here to see him. Probably had forgotten his existence entirely. Probably wouldn't recognize him if he walked right up to them and offered them a table.

Screw her.

If she wanted the tall, dull, and handsome ignoramus, she could have him. Marco didn't need her. Didn't need anyone.

He caught up with Mr. Seveglia, careful to hide behind a column as he passed the front, shielding himself from the happy couple.

"I have another suggestion," he said.

Mr. Seveglia ducked under the counter and into the center of the ovoid bar. "What's that?"

"No teens," he said. "Keep the place family friendly." He pointed to where Shay and Ryan waited for Josh. "Starting with them."

"Teens are really the worst customers anyway," Mr. Seveglia said, wiping down the freshly washed glasses. "Kick them to the curb and put a sign out. We'll bring in the good people—the drinkers." He winked.

Mr. Seveglia was a sick bastard.

Marco told Josh the new plan and instructed him to start with Shay and her boyfriend. He suggested Josh bring the grill cook, Jerome, out with him for extra muscle.

Then Marco got the sandwich board sign from the janitorial closet and wrote: "Families Welcome! Bring Your
Food to Us! We'll Provide the Fun!" It sounded like the
kind of thing his parents would have liked.

He was reminded that he hadn't spoken to his family
today—he'd been calling home every morning before his
mom left for her shift and when his dad would be in from
the night cab run. Marco picked up the phone in the back
of the restaurant near the kitchen and found the line dead.
So he was truly alone now. Not that it changed anything.
Marco was good at alone. He was a survivor. He'd make
it through this.

R
Y
A
N

wesome. It was the only thing running through Ryan's brain. *Awesome. Awesome.* Who cared that they got shut out of the Grill'n'Shake? Just the sight of Shay—skimming a paperback down the aisle from him, his paper flower tucked behind her ear—made him smile. She was the most beautiful person he'd ever seen, and it wasn't just her body (which he wanted, even now that she'd put back on the flowy overshirt). Her light shone on everything around her. The mall was beautiful. He was the guy he'd always wanted to be. Dangerous things were made safe. He could pick up a book and not be afraid to say he didn't get it. When he asked who Jane Austen was, glancing at the book she'd been flipping through, she tapped him on the head with *Pride & Prejudice* and told him to educate himself. Then she held his cheeks in her palms and asked him what he'd been doing all these years in school anyway.

"Football," he'd answered.

Jane Austen was hard. The sentences were long and the story seemed to be about a bunch of girls who wanted to get married. Not exactly the kind of stuff Ryan would have picked up on his own.

"You like this book?" he asked Shay, walking toward her.

"Everyone likes that book," she said. She glanced at where he'd stopped reading. "See, it's actually really funny. Here, Mr. Bennet just played a trick on his wife by going to visit this new guy in town when he'd sort of tortured her by saying he wouldn't go."

"Why didn't she just go herself?" The whole thing seemed way too complicated, and he was only on chapter two.

"A lady can't just run up to any old gentleman and introduce herself!" she exclaimed in that stuffy British voice. Ryan had the feeling he'd be doing a lot better in English if he had someone like Shay to study with.

Shay pulled a book called *The Chocolate War* off a shelf. "Here," she said, taking the Austen from his hands. "This is about surviving an all-boys school. There are even football games in it."

Now this seemed a little closer to Ryan's corner of the universe.

Ryan bought himself the book and Shay bought *how i live now.* "I feel like I need to read this again," she said.

Ryan noticed that she said *again,* meaning she'd read the book before. He was hanging out with a girl who not only read books, but read them more than once.

They stepped out of the bookstore and Ryan wondered

what he should suggest doing next. He had spent his last five bucks on the book, so any options that cost money were out, but he didn't want her to go. He'd left Mike and Drew in the morning allegedly to find a phone so he could call Thad, but had found Shay in the food court instead. Seeing her, he'd forgotten all about the phone, Thad, everything. But all that came rushing back to him when he saw his two friends tromping down the hallway. The palm tree was instantly reminded of its roots.

"J. Shrimp!" Drew shouted, holding his arms out. "We've been looking all over for you."

Mike eyed Shay in a way that made Ryan uncomfortable. "Who's the lady friend?"

Ryan took Shay's hand. "She's my girlfriend," he said.

Shay looked up at him with a smile that made everything else in the universe seem dull in comparison.

"I'm Shaila Dixit," she said, holding out her free hand.

Mike shook it. "A little formal," he said. He looked at Ryan, smiled, and let go of her hand. "But any friend of Ryan's is a pal of mine."

"Dude," Drew said, "tell him. We have ten minutes."

Mike gave Shay the once-over again, then pulled them both into a corner. "We caught up with some boosters who saw the game Sunday," he said. "They're planning an escape through the garage. You in?"

Ryan's first thought was, *Yes, of course*. But then he remembered that escaping would mean leaving Shay, maybe forever. He hadn't even known her full name until she'd said it moments before. How would he ever find her again?

"Come with us," Ryan said, taking her other hand.

"I can't leave without my grandmother and sister."

Shay seemed suddenly more nervous, like she'd just remembered that she had a grandmother and sister.

"Fine," Mike said. "Bring the old lady and the sister. If she's cute she can ride in my car."

"She's ten," Shay said, frowning.

Ryan squeezed Shay's hands. He didn't want her to frown. "Meet me in the parking garage," he said. "Promise?"

Shay smiled again and Ryan had to press his lips to hers, drink her in before she was gone. It was like kissing a star: He felt her light inside him.

She pulled away, slowly. "I'll be there as soon as I find them." She squeezed his hands and ran down the hall toward the escalator.

"Let's move," Mike said, pushing Ryan toward the elevator.

There was a little TV screen in the elevator, which someone had tuned to the local news station. As the three rode to the parking garage level, the news lady yakked about nothing.

"We have former police chief Patrick MacNeil in the studio. Is it true, Chief MacNeil, that given the length of the confinement and blackout of communication from inside the mall that this is not a hostage situation, but more likely a dirty bomb, and, if so, is there any danger for the surrounding community?"

The feed cut out.

"What the . . . ?" Drew said, banging on the screen.

The elevator reached the parking level. The doors opened and the screen switched to say "Have a Nice Day!"

"Must have just been that channel," Ryan said.

"First the phones, now the news. You see a pattern? It won't matter once we get out of here," Mike said, stepping into the gloom of the parking garage.

Three older guys, some who looked older than Ryan's dad, stood under a fluorescent light near a red Suburban. Mike walked up to one and shook his hand.

"Mr. Reynolds," Mike said, "this is Ryan Murphy, the kid I was telling you about."

Mr. Reynolds had slick silver hair and a tanned face. "Saw you play Sunday," he said. "Fierce like your brother, eh?"

"Yes, sir," Ryan said.

Something about Mr. Reynolds's smile and the way he said *fierce,* as if anything less than fierce was wussy, made Ryan nervous.

"What's the play?" Drew asked, smacking his fist into his hand, which was Drew's "ready" pose.

Mr. Reynolds patted the side of the Suburban. "This here is the play."

The plan was to get as far from the main exit ramp as possible, then gun the Suburban's engine and fly into the metal-mesh security gate that had been pulled over the parking garage's opening. The mesh was covered over on the outside by what looked like a giant garbage bag. Mr. Reynolds figured that the gate couldn't stand up to a beating from his truck. He expected to blow through it and drive his way to freedom.

Ryan glanced at the central pavilion, where the escalators to the first floor were. How long would it take Shay?

"Are we all riding in the Suburban?" one of the other

men asked. He glanced at a nice Audi coupe parked two aisles over. "I'd hate to leave her here."

"No, we caravan," Mr. Reynolds said. "I checked out all the windows I could find to gather intel on what we'd face beyond the doors. There are only a couple of police cars on the mall grounds, aside from the big tent where those medical guys in the suits are working. But it's the wall they've built around the grounds that I'm worried about. They've got a perimeter established to keep the press back.

"If we're in a couple of cars going through the gate, though, we can split up on the outside. With more targets, they'll have a harder time stopping any one of us. I think that's our best shot at getting out."

The plan sounded solid—excitement buzzed through Ryan. He checked the pavilion. Still empty.

The men began to split up.

Mike pulled out a set of keys. "Let's move, J. Shrimp."

"Shay's not here yet," Ryan said.

Drew smacked the back of Ryan's head. "Dude, it's now or never."

Mike sighed. "You can wait for her while I get the car," he said, "but if she's not here by the time I get back, you've got to let her go." He loped across the pavement toward his car, which beeped as he pressed a button on his key ring. Drew followed, calling shotgun.

Ryan stared at the pavilion, willing Shay to appear. *Please, god, let her come with us.* He saw feet on the escalator. His heart leaped. But it was just some old dude. He stepped out and walked to a sedan parked nearby.

Mike pulled in front of Ryan. "Time to man up, J. Shrimp," he said through the open window.

"She's coming," Ryan said. Had the kiss been too much? Had he scared her off?

Drew stepped out of the passenger door and pushed forward his seat. "Get in before I have to drag your ass over here."

Ryan checked his watch. It'd been twenty minutes. She might still be coming.

Drew grabbed his arm and pulled him to the passenger door. "Forget the bitch," he said, shoving Ryan into the back.

Ryan glanced one more time at the empty pavilion as Mike's car revved down the aisle and pulled up behind the Audi. They had to move quickly; Mr. Reynolds was afraid the engine noise would attract attention. Their cars were started; they had to do it or give up. Mr. Reynolds didn't seem like the kind of man to give up on anything.

For those brief moments, as the cars grumbled near the wall, Ryan felt the full extent of the insanity of this plan as an urgent need to pee. He had to get out of that car and use a bathroom. He needed to think about this—they were planning on driving at full speed *on purpose* into a wall!

But then the Suburban lurched and squealed down the road between the parked cars. Mike floored it and the M3 bolted after the Audi. Ryan's heart raced; exhilaration at the sheer speed of their attack flooded through him. He remembered, in the last second, that he hadn't buckled his seat belt and reached for the strap. The seat belt locked just before the Suburban hit the gate.

Ryan had not been prepared for what happened next: Complete and total failure.

The Suburban smashed into the gate, but the gate held. It must have been reinforced on the outside by something incredibly strong—the metal-mesh didn't move an inch.

The back end of Mr. Reynolds's truck shot up into the air, then bounced down hard. The Audi squealed out of the way and flipped over, rolling into a parked minivan. Mike managed to veer off course down an aisle and slammed on the brakes. Ryan was thrown forward, but was held against the leather of the seat by his belt. Mike too remained seated. Drew, however, had not put on his belt; he slammed into the windshield, spiderwebbing the glass.

"Dude!" Mike said, pulling Drew back into his seat.

Drew put his hand to his head. "It's cool," he said. He lifted his hand, removing a splinter of glass from his scalp. Blood trickled down his face.

Mike punched him in the arm. "I always tell you to put your goddamned belt on!" He sounded scared.

Ryan felt tingly all over, like maybe he'd been tossed from his own body. But he was all right. By some small miracle, they were all okay.

A cop came running toward them. "Anyone hurt?" he asked, breathing hard. He must have run the whole way down.

"No, sir," Mike said. He spoke in a quiet voice Ryan had never heard him use before.

The cop ran toward the Audi and Suburban without so much as a nod good-bye. An arm hung off the side of the Suburban's hood—they were not all okay.

Other people rushed out of the central pavilion. Ryan guessed the noise from the crash had spooked the whole mall.

Several guards broke out of the crowd. A few stood in front of the onlookers, keeping them from getting any closer. The rest ran past the M3 to the other cars. They dragged Mr. Reynolds out of his Suburban. Some hazmat guys rushed by pushing a gurney.

The guards knocked together a jail from some fencing material brought down from the HomeMart. Ryan, Mike, Drew, and the Audi guy were tossed into the cages. After being released from the medical ward, Mr. Reynolds joined them. His neck was in a brace. The guy who'd been riding with Mr. Reynolds was in critical condition.

"It'll be all right, boys," Mr. Reynolds said as the guard closed the gate on his cell. "I'll figure a way to get us out of this. No way I'm taking part in this government-run experiment."

"I'll bust a skull before I let them suck out my DNA," Mike growled.

All Ryan could think was that he was lucky to be alive. And even if he was in jail, he was also still in the mall. Maybe Shay would find him, help to get him out. With her, such things felt possible. He leaned against the fence, pulled out her book, and pretended she was there reading with him.

DAY
FIVE

· WEDNESDAY ·

LEXI

The glare of Lights On burned through Lexi's eyelids. She felt as if she were made of mist; she hadn't gotten much in the way of sleep. From the sound of it, Ginger hadn't slept much either. The throw pillow pile in JCPenney was more comfortable than the cement floor of the Apple Store, but last night's CB call had changed something. Suddenly the divide between them and everyone outside seemed insurmountable.

She'd hidden the portable CB under the bottom shelf against the wall. No one would find it there; even vacuums had forgotten that particular span of floor, judging from the herd of dust bunnies wafting around.

The mall speakers crackled to life. "Alexandra Ross, please report to the Apple Store." The Senator's voice was a barely controlled scream.

Ginger pushed herself to sitting. She glanced at Lexi

and smiled weakly. "I guess we're not getting breakfast together."

The oil slick in Lexi's gut returned, seeping in under the nauseating lightness.

"No," Lexi said. She stood, zipped her hoodie. She felt cold.

Ginger grabbed her hand. "Thank you," she said. "For helping me talk to my dad."

Lexi let her go. "No problem," she said.

Ginger stood beside her. "I guess I should retrieve Maddie."

"Yeah."

"We'll catch up with you later?"

"Sure."

Ginger picked up her purse, rummaged through it, and pulled out a tiny bottle of scented hand sanitizer. "Going to need more of this," she said, squeezing the last of the bottle into her palms.

"You can't tell anyone what I told you," Lexi said. "Not even Maddie, okay?" It was like tossing water on the ashes after the house had already burned.

Ginger slid a pink-painted nail in an X over her heart. "Our secret."

Lexi tried to come up with the likely reasons for her mother to scream her name over a loudspeaker at eight in the morning. Had she heard about the shoplifting? The stunt at the bowling alley? Was she angry that Lexi had not returned to the Apple Store last night? She couldn't have found out about Ginger's call. Lexi had been with

Ginger all night. Unless Ginger's dad had done something. The oil slick in her gut confirmed it—Ginger's dad had done something. *What?*

She hovered outside the entrance to the Apple Store. Her mother was near the registers in the back talking to Dad. The Senator was whispering loudly, slicing her hands through the air. Dad was nodding, hand on chin.

Lexi took a deep breath and stepped into the store.

The Senator's eyes locked onto her. "The stockroom," she said, turning.

Dad was right behind her. Neither waited to see if Lexi followed.

Lexi felt sweat prick out all over her skin. Even if Ginger's dad did something, how could they have linked anything back to her?

Her parents were waiting in the back corner. There was a makeshift lounge back there—a threadbare couch, some chairs, a mini fridge. The Senator and Arthur stood in front of a flimsy table.

"I trusted you," her mother growled. "It's clear now that was my first mistake."

Lexi flinched as if smacked.

"How did you call Darren?" her father asked calmly.

So that was how they'd found her out.

"I knew Darren had a CB radio. I called him using that. Ginger was freaking out and was desperate to talk to her dad."

"This radio?" The Senator pulled the police scanner from her pocket.

Lexi didn't correct her mistake.

"Why was Ginger freaking out, might I ask?"

"I told her. Not everything, just that there was a sickness."

"And that we were curing it?"

"I didn't want her to worry."

The Senator snorted a nasty laugh. "Well, I'm glad you calmed her fears. They've determined it's the flu, meaning there is no cure."

The flu? That didn't sound too devastating.

Dad glared at the Senator, then turned back to Lexi. "Your mother told you about the bomb in secret for a reason," he said. "She's trying to keep a lot of already frightened people from panicking. You saw the riot two nights ago. That is exactly the kind of situation we're trying to avoid repeating."

His calm, scolding tone infuriated her.

"People need to know about the flu," Lexi said. "Why not just tell people to wear face masks? Wash their hands? No one's protecting themselves because they don't know that they should. And if it's just a flu strain, why not let us all out? People get the flu all the time."

The Senator threw her hands up. "Oh, so now you're in charge of this situation?"

"At least I'd keep people from playing spin the bottle when they could be spreading disease with every kiss!"

"You started a riot!" the Senator shouted. "On the outside. Hundreds of people, more every hour, are picketing and screaming at the barriers surrounding the mall. The governor's called in the National Guard. This is exactly why the Feds shut down the Internet and the phones.

They did not want the people outside to worry until we knew what we were dealing with."

This is not all my fault. It couldn't be all her fault.

Lexi folded her arms across her chest. "You expected people's families to just sit around and wait for you to spoon-feed them whatever lies you wanted?"

The Senator slapped Lexi across the face.

"Dorothy!" Dad shouted.

"Wake up," the Senator said, ignoring Arthur. "This is not some battle of wills between you and me. This is a real crisis. I have the president himself inquiring into whether my daughter could be a part of whatever organization put this bomb here in the first place."

The icy claws strangled Lexi once again.

The Senator continued. "Now you're starting to get it. We turned the news channels off in the mall so people couldn't see their grandparents, parents, children being driven away from the perimeter by armed soldiers. Darren's been taken in for questioning. The FBI is doing a background check into all our finances and scouring your computers at home to look for connections to terrorist organizations. This is all really happening."

Lexi felt like a balloon whose string had been cut. She felt suddenly free. "So you're saying my life is trashed?"

Arthur stepped in front of the Senator. "Lex, your mother is just trying—"

"Trying to say that my life is trashed." Lexi stood straighter. "Good. I barely had a life on the outside anyway, right?"

"Don't you get mouthy with me," the Senator snarled.

"I'll do what I want," Lexi said, turning.

The police scanner flew by her head and exploded against the wall.

"Don't you walk away from me!" the Senator screamed.

Lexi walked faster, ran out of the stockroom, out of the Apple Store, tears streaming down her cheeks. There was only one place to go. She stomped up the stairs and loped toward the Abercrombie. Ginger was coming out of the entrance. She was crying too.

"She's sick!" Ginger yelped. "Maddie's sick, and so are a couple other kids. I was so scared, I just ran out."

She'd been right. Those kids had been playing Russian roulette. And Maddie had lost.

It was clear what Lexi had to do. She had to take care of whomever she could, starting with Maddie and the other kids in the Abercrombie. So she'd have to spill a few more Ross Family Secrets; it's not like her mother could get any angrier.

"Come with me," she said to Ginger.

Ginger followed, hands clasped in front of her. "Shouldn't we get help? Get one of those space people?"

Lexi gritted her jaw. "The *government* is only interested in covering their ass. The medical teams would probably lock those kids up for observation instead of treating whatever's wrong with them."

Ginger stopped. "So, what? *You're* going to save them?"

Lexi faced her. "It doesn't look like there's anyone else to do the job. Come on, we can get supplies."

"No." Ginger seemed to shrink into herself. "I mean, I'll help you get supplies, but I'm not going back in there."

"What do you mean?" Lexi cocked her head. "Maddie's your best friend."

Ginger stepped back. "She's sick," she said, stepping farther away. "I'm sorry."

Lexi's heart raced. She was truly alone.

"Coward," Lexi said. She left Ginger standing in the hallway.

She would not abandon those kids. It was just the flu. She could help them. Even if her mother wouldn't.

Lexi went into the PhreshPharm and picked up a basket. She knocked bottles of flu medicine, vitamin C, echinacea, Tylenol, and instant cold packs into it. There were some cans of chicken soup in another aisle; she grabbed those and a flimsy-looking can opener. Then she snagged the biggest bottle of hand sanitizer she could and all the face masks they had on the shelves—for woodworking, disease, whatever.

She dragged everything to the checkout counter. The clerk began unloading the basket and ringing things up.

"You know something I don't?" the person said, sliding the huge bottle of hand sanitizer into a bag.

Lexi handed over a wad of cash—all her money—and grabbed the bags.

"Wash your hands," she said.

MARCO

Sorry, we don't have any waffles left," Marco said, cringing. People were getting pissed. One guy had picked up his fork and threatened to sample Marco's arm if he didn't dig a piece of bacon out of some corner somewhere.

This woman simply sagged in her seat. "Well, then bring me whatever's left that I can put syrup on."

Marco flipped open his order pad—he'd written down all the breakfast items that remained in the freezer. "Toast?"

"Fine," the woman said, hugging her purse to her belly. "All I wanted was a new pair of loafers," she said, apropos of nothing. "Imagine, if only I'd waited until Sunday, none of this would have happened."

Marco wasn't sure what to say. The quarantine still would have happened, just not to her.

"Sorry," he muttered, thinking that was the response most likely to get him a tip.

She didn't respond. The lady stared at the wall across the aisle, breathing softly.

The guy this morning who wouldn't take *no bacon* for an answer was not the first to threaten Marco with his utensil. And Jerome had to take over as bathroom guard after a guy picked Josh up and tossed him out of the way rather than pay the twenty-five cents to use the john. Jerome was not someone any mall-walker was likely to mess with.

Marco's world was now divided between the mall-walkers and the mall-workers. Of course, there were the Outsiders, who were a special class, the overlords of this insane little petri dish, but the rest were either mall-workers, suffering on, running the stores, cleaning up the mess, or mall-walkers with nothing to do but hang out, flirt, see movies, window-shop, whatever. Marco was beginning to really hate the mall-walkers. All they did was whine and complain. They should try pulling six straight shifts. They should shut the hell up and be grateful anyone's serving them at all.

With the rising emotional barometer, Marco began to consider whether there was any possible scenario for survival within the mall. Each new malevolent customer made escape seem the best option. But was it even possible?

He'd heard some kids talking about the escape attempt through the parking garage. You didn't need tarot cards to predict the failure of that attempt. If the Outsiders had blocked even the obscure fire escape in its ceiling, surely they would have considered the possibility of someone driving their car through the garage's security gate. Anyone who'd ever seen an action movie could have called that plan.

He needed to think of something truly insane, something not even Michael Bay had conceived of doing. Something beyond the thinking of J. J. Abrams.

"Kid!"

A guy at table ten was waving an empty coffee mug at Marco. *Yeah, buddy, get in line.* They were rationing coffee now. Mr. Seveglia sprinkled the new grinds into the machine over the old to give the water some color. Marco imagined the resulting liquid tasted somewhere between burnt dirt and pond scum. He stalked up to the coffeemaker and grabbed the pot, then tromped back to the guy at ten and gave him a half cup.

"Fill 'er up, kid," the guy said. "I haven't slept since Friday."

Marco braced himself. "Sorry," he said. "We're only allowed to do one half-cup refill per order. If you want a full cup, you have to pay for another."

The man looked at the sad, tannish water in the mug. Marco waited for him to chuck it at the wall. But the man simply slurped his ration down.

"I'll take another order, then." He held up the empty cup. He looked like he was ready to cry. A guy who was, like, Marco's dad's age. On the verge of tears over coffee.

Marco had to get out of the mall. He couldn't take this anymore.

He filled the guy's mug and the other empty cup on the table. "Don't tell," he said.

The guy smiled weakly. "You're a good kid," he said.

Marco nodded and walked quickly away, reminding himself that he hated these people.

Toward the end of the breakfast rush, two security guards walked in through the back entrance and approached the server station. Josh was crouched against the wall holding a bag of ice to his shoulder—he'd pulled something lifting a bin full of dirty dishes. If things kept up this way, Marco and Josh would have to be taped together to function.

Marco hopped off the stool and grabbed two menus from the side of the server stand. "I'll take these guys."

Josh didn't even look up.

The guards wanted to sit in the back, away from the hallway. It didn't matter to Marco, so he sat them in a booth in the back corner. As he led them to their seats, they continued their conversation as if he weren't there.

"You see that memo from the Suits?" the one said.

"Don't mention it," the other replied. "You'll ruin my appetite."

"You think it's serious?"

"What kind of sick monkey would put that in a memo as a joke?"

Marco slid the menus onto the tabletop. "We're out of almost everything," he said. He opened his pad and examined the list of what remained. "I think I can do eggs, maybe toast."

The worried guy glanced at Marco. "Two coffees," he said.

"And whatever else they got left back there," the other said. "Two of that."

Marco nodded and gave their order directly to the cook—the computer system was useless now that none of the regular menu items were available. He went to grab the coffee and saw that the pot was empty. Marco needed to brew a new pot, and to do so, he needed more grounds. He checked the bar, but the Enforcer wasn't there. A guy sat alone at the counter, a half-empty beer in his hand, and watched the sitcom being rerun on the TVs. The news channels were all blocked—not that they'd shown more than vapid speculation over the last few days. Marco wondered what had happened to cause the government to cut them off. *Nothing good.*

The door to Mr. Seveglia's office was slightly ajar. Marco knocked, pushing the door open. Mr. Seveglia was slumped over his desk. Marco touched his shoulder. The body slid farther across the desktop, knocking over a glass of water.

Marco ran out to the dishwashing sink and washed his hands. He didn't know why he was so shocked; Seveglia had been hacking like crazy. But damn. He had to think. He had to tell someone. But what if everyone just panicked and left him alone with this dead guy and the surly customers? No, he needed a plan before he broke this bombshell. First, he had to make coffee. Coffee. *Yes. Make the coffee.* He needed time to plan.

Marco went back to the office, opened the door, used his apron to grab the keys from the desk, and shut the door quietly behind him. Then he grabbed coffee from the locked bar cabinet and returned to the machine. Everything would be fine. He would think of something. He wiped his face on his sleeve. When the pot was full, he returned to the guards.

They didn't see him as he approached; otherwise Marco was sure they would have shut their mouths.

"But how can a flu be deadly?" the worried guy said. "Isn't the flu just, well, the flu?"

Marco ducked into the nearest booth and sunk below the dividing wall so he could eavesdrop.

"You heard of the Spanish flu? Killed millions of people," the other guy said.

"But that was a hundred years ago," Worrier said.

"That's the thing about flus," the other guy said. "There's no cure for a flu virus, only natural immunity. The Suits explained that when a flu mutates, no one has immunity and it's a potential pandemic. Nothing they can do about it."

"But to quarantine this place indefinitely?" Worrier said.

"Better than letting it spread," the other guy said. "Plus, we get overtime on top of the bonus."

"Quarantined," Worried repeated, as if letting his own words sink in. "These people are going to eat each other alive."

Marco stood and went to the cops' table. He tried to control the tremors running throughout his body as he poured their coffee. "Your orders should be out soon," he said.

The worrier cop waved his hand at Marco, as if to say who cared when the food came.

This was exactly Marco's thought on the issue. What

else mattered besides getting out of here before being killed by either choice a, the flu, or choice b, the other inmates?

Nothing else mattered.

Marco left the coffeepot on the server stand and untied his apron. He tossed it at Josh.

"The place is yours," he said.

Josh looked at the apron, then at Marco. "Dude," he said. "Not you too."

"Good luck," Marco said. And he meant it.

The guards had given him an idea—if they came in through the back, they had universal card keys, meaning they could open any service door in the mall. Marco needed one of those keys. Once he had it, he could search every corner of this place for an exit. There had to be a way out. And Marco would be the one to find it.

R Y A N

Ryan had never read so much in his life: two books in as many days. All it took was being jailed in a mall. *The Chocolate War* made him uncomfortable, as if Shay were accusing him of being no better than the assholes in this book—even though she knew nothing about his smashing the Tarrytown guy's face. Would she be scared of him if she knew? That cold pleasure he'd felt made him sick. He didn't want to be scary.

"I need a bathroom," Mike said, kicking the fence.

"Quiet down," the cop on duty shouted. "Just use the corner farthest from where you sleep."

The cops were useless. They changed every few hours and none offered a shred of information. How long would they be held in these cages? Was there going to be some trial? The guards shrugged off every question. They just sat in the folding chair near Mr. Reynolds's cell and read their magazines.

"You boys have any cell signal?" the Audi guy asked.

"They shut down the towers days ago," Mike said.

"Why would they shut down the cell towers?" Drew asked.

"To keep us from talking to people on the outside," Mr. Reynolds said, his voice low and grumbling. "That's just like these government people. They don't want our families to know we're being caged like a bunch of rats." He yelled the last few words in the cop's direction.

The cop just turned the page and slurped his coffee.

Ryan couldn't get warm. His head hurt. He crawled to where Drew and Mike sat in the back corner. The two were huddled together, mumbling.

"What's up?" he asked.

Mike looked at him. "Nothing," he said. "Yet." He turned his head back to Drew.

The Audi guy coughed loudly. He'd been coughing and snotting up a storm all morning. He must have had some cold. Ryan hoped he hadn't caught it. "Hey," Audi shouted in a gravelly voice, his head turned toward the cop. "I need some water."

"Meal's in an hour," the cop grunted back.

Audi coughed again. This time, the coughing went on for a while. He seemed like he couldn't get a breath. He coughed and then gasped and then coughed some more.

Ryan had never seen anyone cough like that. "He needs some water!" he shouted.

The cop looked up. The Audi guy fell to his knees. He was still coughing. His fingernails were bluish. *Was it from gripping the pavement?*

Ryan wanted to run. He was ready to claw through the

walls to get away from that coughing. What was wrong with this guy? Then he felt a tickle in his own throat. He swallowed.

The cop picked up his walkie-talkie and mumbled something into it, then lugged his fat ass out of the chair and began fumbling for the keys to the Audi guy's cell. Mike grabbed Ryan's arm and pulled him against the wall farthest from the Audi guy.

Audi was on the floor now. The coughing had stopped. He was kind of whining. He sounded like a sad dog. Ryan was frozen where he stood on the cement.

The cop got the cage open and ran to the Audi guy. "Hey," the cop said, shaking him.

This disturbance brought on another fit of coughing. The cop had to lean away from Audi, he was thrashing so badly with each hacking cough. His hands were blue now. When he opened his eyes to gasp for breath, they were red—not bloodshot, all red. Then he coughed up some bloody, foamy spit.

The cop jumped back. "What in the name—"

A guy in a hazmat suit pulled the cop out of the way. Ryan saw that a whole team of medical guys had appeared in front of the row of cells.

The hazmat guy injected Audi with something, and he fell limp. Another grabbed Audi's legs, and the two of them lifted him onto a gurney.

"We'll send another team down," the hazmat guy said to the cop. "We've got to isolate these individuals."

The cop seemed as freaked out as Ryan felt. He nodded and shut the cage door.

The hazmat guy gave the four of them the once-over.

"You all appear asymptomatic, so you should be all right for the time being. We'll be back to move you to the medical ward for observation."

No matter how crappy he felt, Ryan was not going anywhere with that hazmat guy.

"Shrimp," Mike barked, as if answering Ryan's plea.

Ryan dragged himself to the back corner.

Mike pushed on the fencing; the mesh bent back, creating an opening a little over a foot wide. They'd undone the wires that held the cage together. "Just big enough for a Jumbo Shrimp to fit through," Mike said. He raised his eyebrows and cocked his head toward the hole.

"What about you guys?" Ryan asked.

Drew smacked him on the back of the head. "You get out and filch the keys, then let us all out."

"How am I supposed to get the keys?" Ryan asked.

Mike pulled Ryan's collar, dragging his head down to hiss in his ear. "I want a clean hit, right in the gut," he said. "Just like we do a hundred times every practice. You'll knock the old bag right out."

Mike let go of him and Ryan stumbled back onto his ass. *Tackle a cop?* Ryan glanced over his shoulder at the floor of Audi's cage. A little puddle of bloody drool congealed on the cement where Audi had collapsed.

Ryan did not want to be moved to the medical ward.

"Okay," he said.

They waited until they were sure the cop was not looking, then Mike and Drew pushed on the fencing. The hole opened up and Ryan shoved himself through the gap. The metal edges of the links scraped at his shoulders, but he managed to drag himself out onto the pavement.

He was free. He could just run. *Not even an option.*

Mike jerked his head at the row of parked cars. Ryan dashed to hide behind a minivan's bumper.

Drew strode to the front of his cage and began to rattle the door.

"Yo!" he shouted. "I want out of here before that asshole comes back."

"Shut up," Mike said, walking up to Drew.

"You shut up," Drew said, shoving Mike.

Mike shoved him back and then one of them was thrown against the cage wall, shaking the whole jail. That got the cop up.

"You boys quit it," he said, groaning as he got up out of the chair. He began to walk along the front of the cages toward Mike and Drew.

This was the moment. Ryan sprang from behind the minivan and charged at full-speed. He dropped his shoulder and hit the cop square in the gut. The guy popped air from his lungs and fell flat on the pavement. His head hit the cement and he was out.

Ryan stood. It'd been a clean tackle.

"Hey!" Another cop appeared out of the shadows.

"The keys!" Drew shouted.

Ryan pulled the keys from the cop's pocket and passed them to Mike. Then he hefted the downed cop's radio and threw a pass directly into the advancing cop's skull. The guy dropped like a tackle bag.

What have I done?

"Hells yeah, J. Shrimp!" Drew howled.

Mike burst out of the cage. He knelt beside the cop and patted him down. The cop groaned.

"He'll be fine," Mike said, tucking something into his jeans.

The ding of an elevator opening its doors echoed throughout the garage. *The medical team . . .*

"Kid!" shouted Mr. Reynolds. He held his hands up.

Mike chucked the keys over the fence wall and Mr. Reynolds caught them. Then Mike took off toward the central pavilion.

Drew and Ryan bolted down the pavement after him.

S H A Y

"Can I have another ice chip?" Preeti asked, her voice muffled by her stuffed and running nose.

Shay spooned a sliver from the cup in her hands, lifted Preeti's face mask, and dropped the ice onto her sister's tongue. Preeti groaned and rolled over. In the other bed lay Nani. She coughed violently, then fell back into a sleep like death. The skin around her lips was cracked and peeling. Her ears and fingertips were turning blue just like the woman who'd died. Shay had pulled the sheet up to hide them from Preeti.

After leaving Ryan, she'd raced back to the Snooze-Select, heart bursting at the thought of getting out of the mall with him. When she got there, Nani's bed was empty. On the comforter was a note in Preeti's loopy, little-girl scrawl that read: "Called spacemen. Sick." Shay had bolted down the halls, pushed past dawdlers on the escalator, and burst screaming into the EMC. The senator had taken her back to where her family lay on neighboring deathbeds.

As much as the hazmat-suited doctors pretended to give a crap about Preeti and Nani, Shay could tell they couldn't care less about her family's survival. Every hour or so, someone would poke their tented head through the curtains, but only to ensure that the machines were all beeping properly. Not so at her mother's hospital. If they could just get the hell out of here, Shay knew that Ba could save them.

But how to escape? Ryan was long gone. Nani's car was in the outdoor lot. All Shay had was a piece of information, something the senator would not like let out of the bag.

Shay put the cup of ice on the metal tray between the two beds and exited the curtain-room. She grabbed a hazmat suit by the sleeve.

"I need the senator," she said.

The suit turned. The man picked her fingers from the plastic. "Please don't pull the fabric," he said. "The senator is helping other patients. She'll see you when she's available."

She'll see me now or she'll regret it.

Shay began a room by room search for the woman. As she neared the front, she saw her step out of a curtain-room.

"Senator," Shay stated. "I have to speak with you."

The woman looked worn out. Her suit was wrinkled. A piece of hair stuck out at an awkward angle. Her dark skin had an ashy tone. But her eyes were fierce as a tiger's. "Miss Dixit, there's a bit of a line."

"I know you're the reason we're all stuck in here." Shay felt rather ferocious herself.

The senator stood straighter. "I'm not sure what you think you know, Shaila, but I'm happy to hear what you have to say."

"I have a proposition." Shay swallowed. "You get my grandmother and sister out of here and to my mother's hospital and I won't tell people that it was your screwup that got us all quarantined in the first place."

The senator's face softened. Shay wanted to punch that face with its look of pity.

"Miss Dixit," the senator said, placing her hand on Shay's shoulder. "Even if I could get your grandmother and sister out, I would not do it. Yes, you're right, it was my call originally to lock down the mall, and that was technically against protocol. But protocol is being altered as we speak, given the gravity of our current situation, and I doubt you could find many outside the mall to support your claims of wrongful imprisonment.

"I understand that you are upset and worried, but that is really no excuse for extortion and I would appreciate you thinking more carefully before attempting to blackmail a public official. It is, after all, a crime."

The senator squeezed her shoulder and walked away.

Shay felt like a husk, like her soul had flown free quite some time ago. She had to get out. Get away. There had to be a way out.

She needed an ally, a friend, a coconspirator. Ryan had mentioned that Marco had tried to help him escape. Maybe he could help her. Maybe together, they could come up with some previously inconceivable route out.

Shay checked back in on Preeti and Nani. No change—Preeti slept, Nani coughed. *I will get you out of here.*

She grabbed her bag and legged it for the Grill'n'Shake. By some lucky twist of fate, Marco was leaving the restaurant just as she approached.

"Hey!" she yelled, putting on her friendliest face and giving him a big wave.

Marco froze for a second, glared at her. "What do you want?"

Shay wasn't sure why he was so cold. It didn't matter. Whatever the reason, she had to turn things around. "Just the person I was looking for!" she said, smiling wide.

His shoulders relaxed slightly. "Really?"

She threw her arms around him. "Really," she said. It felt good to hold a body.

Marco stiffened in her embrace and she let him go.

"Sorry," she said. "I'm all messed up. Nani's sick. So is Preeti."

"Sick how?"

Shay felt tears bloat her eyelids. "The doctors won't say anything. They're both just sick with like the worst cold ever."

"It's not a cold," Marco said. He waved her over to a bench in the corner, away from the crowds. "It's the flu. A killer flu, like in the movies."

It was as if she'd known all along. "The bomb?"

He nodded. "We have to get out of here," he said.

"That is exactly why I came up here," she said, relieved he'd brought it up, relieved that maybe he'd already worked out the method of their escape. "So how do we do it?" she asked.

Marco leaned back on the bench, raked his fingers through his hair. "I'm working on it."

Shay held her head in her hands. There had to be some way out. *Think, think.*

Somewhere, off to her left, a woman dropped to the floor, taking a metal stand of whirligigs down with her. The people around her backed away. The woman began to wheeze and suck air, like she was choking. A security guard used his walkie-talkie, and a hazmat guy arrived within minutes with a stretcher. He loaded the woman onto it and took her away. As soon as she was gone, the crowd began to flow again. The merchant picked up the stand, rearranged the whirligigs. It was like nothing had ever happened.

"The EMC," Shay said. "In the PaperClips. The hazmat people have to be going in and out from somewhere in there."

Marco sat up. "We could sneak in through the service corridor, leave without them even knowing we were there."

"You have a key?" Shay leaned toward him.

"No," he said. "But I know where we can get one."

They sat outside the Grill'n'Shake and watched for the two guards Marco had served earlier. After a half hour, they emerged and trotted toward the elevators.

Shay and Marco watched them sink down the glass-enclosed shaft, saw them travel all the way down past the first floor.

"The parking garage," Marco said.

They followed the officers down in the next elevator. The garage was mostly empty. Toward the back wall, they heard voices, the bleat of a walkie-talkie. Marco motioned to her, and they slunk along behind the parked cars toward the rear wall.

Some makeshift cages of chain-link fencing stood along the wall. The two guards they'd followed were leaning over the prone body of a cop.

"He's breathing," one guard said.

"Those demolition derby assholes did this," the other said. "I will make them pay."

The first guard patted his partner's shoulder. "Let's get him to the Suits."

They picked up their friend by the arms and legs and carried him back toward the elevator.

"What do we do now?" Shay whispered.

Marco held a finger to his lips. Then he pointed at a shadow beyond the cages: Another downed guard.

Once the two had carried their friend to the elevator, Marco and Shay crept up to the guard lying in the shadows. A walkie-talkie lay next to him. A thin dribble of blood ran from the corner of his mouth.

"Is he dead?" Shay asked.

Marco seemed less sure of himself. Then he sighed. "He breathed," he said, pointing. "I saw his chest move."

"And how is he going to help us?" Shay asked.

"He isn't," Marco said. He began patting around the guy's belt. He emerged with a card key. "This is."

Marco explained that all the security doors were controlled by card keys—he showed her the one from his wallet. The mall cops had a special card key that, unlike his, could open any door in the mall.

Hope spread like warmth throughout her empty body. "We're on our way," she said.

"Wait," he said. He picked up the walkie-talkie and pushed the TALK button. "Second man down in the parking garage."

A voice responded, acknowledging the call. "Sending a team."

Marco then turned the volume way down and pocketed the thing. "Just in case," he said.

He'd get no argument from Shay.

As they neared the medical ward, Shay laid out her plan for getting Preeti and Nani out of the EMC.

Marco scowled. "You never mentioned getting them out too," he said.

"They're coming with us or I scream that you have the flu." Shay was utterly serious.

Marco held up his hands. "Okay," he said. "Calm yourself. What's your plan?"

"There's a space between the windows and the curtained wall. We get them out the front, then all sneak around to the service hall."

Shay saw doubt on his face. She took his hand and squeezed it. He looked at his hand and blushed. So what if she didn't feel anything? She would get his help whichever way she had to.

Marco shrugged like *what the hell* and followed her into the EMC.

All was not well in the med center. Hazmat suits ran from one side of the curtain complex to the other. Machines beeped and wailed. No one noticed Shay and Marco as they walked into the main area. For a minute, Shay wondered if they needed any plan, whether they might just walk out without anyone paying them any mind.

But then they got to Nani and Preeti's room. Three hazmat suits crowded Nani's bed. Preeti was sitting up, crying.

"What are you doing?" Shay yelled.

The hazmat people parted. Nani lay still but with a huge plastic tube coming out of her mouth. An IV dripped into her arm. A machine attached to the bed pole wheezed rhythmically, pumping air into and out of Nani's lungs.

A hazmat doctor put a hand on Shay's shoulder. "I'm sorry, but your grandmother has not responded to the antiviral medication. She has developed acute respiratory distress syndrome," she said. "We have to move her to our ICU area."

"Can I come?" Shay tried to touch Nani's hand; the doctor caught her fingers.

"We'll let you know if her condition improves."

The doctors wheeled Nani out.

"Why are you always gone?" Preeti cried, her voice catching on a sob.

Tears ran down Shay's cheeks. She hugged her sister. "I'm sorry," she said. "I was trying to get help."

Preeti cried, soaking Shay's choli, until a coughing fit forced her to lie down. She fell into a feverish sleep, mumbling something about spinning. Shay stumbled back. Marco caught her.

"You should go, escape," she said, not looking at him. "I can't leave, not without them."

He stepped around to face her. "If you want me to, I'll stay."

He should leave. He should save himself. But Shay didn't want to be alone. She couldn't handle this alone.

"That would be really nice," she said.

He seemed to be waiting for something.

She lifted herself to her tiptoes and kissed him on the cheek. Her lips felt papery against his skin. But he glowed like she had given him something better than escape.

"Then I'll stay," he said. He sat on the floor and patted the tile next to him. She sat. And when he put his arm around her, she let it stay because any arm was a comfort at this point. Any boy would do.

DAY

SIX

·THURSDAY·

S H A Y

Shay lay on the floor where Nani's bed had stood. Marco was behind her, spooning her. She'd even let him throw an arm over her side. She felt so cold.

Preeti drifted in and out of sleep. The doctors came in every hour and checked her IV drip. They would look down at Shay, see her open eyes, and tell her to get some rest, there was nothing she could do.

Now. There was nothing she could do *now*. But she could have done so much before. If only she'd let herself see what had been happening. Why didn't she put things together? Maybe if she'd left Nani here in the first place, she wouldn't have developed the respiratory distress and wouldn't be sedated and full of tubes and sucking air through a machine. Maybe Preeti wouldn't have gotten sick. *If I hadn't been so pathetically needy, they would have never come to the mall in the first place.*

Marco snored and rolled away from her. Shay felt the cold air tickle her spine. She shifted onto her back and a twinge of pain ran from her hip down her leg. It was a welcome distraction, the pain. At least she felt something.

A white glare blinded her—Lights On.

Marco winced at the ceiling. "They could at least make it gradual," he grumbled. "Like use a dimmer or something."

"I think you should write a letter," Shay said. "Someone should get on that dimmer situation pronto."

Marco rolled onto his side, his face inches from her own. "I see we're cheerful as a cheerleader this morning." He pushed himself up and sat cross-legged. "What if I offered to buy you a dee-licious donut?" He cocked his head and smiled. He had a nice smile.

"How about a smoothie?" Shay said. She saw no reason to stay in the EMC. She was no use to anyone.

"Anything you want," he said, standing. He held his hand out to help her up. She pushed herself to her feet and brushed off her kameez.

"I could really use some clean clothes," Shay muttered, noting a tear in the thin fabric.

"Sure," Marco said, checking his wallet. "I think I have enough."

Shay gave him a shove. "I don't need a sugar daddy."

Nani's purse lay under the metal tray. Shay dug around for Nani's wallet and took out her credit card. She only had the one, for emergencies, she always said. If Shay's current situation was anything, it was most certainly an emergency.

"Let's go shopping," she said.

■ ■ ■

They were pretty much alone in the H&M. No one had tried to help them. No salesperson stood behind the registers.

"How about this shirt?" Marco asked, holding up a slinky-looking spandex tank.

"There are strippers with classier getups," Shay retorted, pulling out something a bit more her. It was a regularish T-shirt, but in a soft cotton knit with a wide neckline to complement her broad shoulders. When she stepped out of the changing room, Marco's face lit up.

"You're right," he said. "That's the right shirt for you."

"I'll get two," she said. If they were going to be here for a while, she might as well have a change of clothes. She tried on some new jeans and boots. She left her old clothes in the dressing room—she never wanted to see those rags again.

Marco seemed perfectly happy watching her flip through the racks. He even let her pick out a jacket for him to try on.

"This would look really great on you," she said, holding it up in front of him. *Really great* was a definite overstatement of the case, but anything would improve his current look of fresh-out-of-the-hamper dishevelment.

Marco took the jacket, looked at the price. "I don't normally do jackets."

"You need that jacket, trust me. I have a crazy idea. Let's put on the clothes and just walk out." Part of her was joking, but once said, she was surprised by how much she really wanted to do it.

Marco looked around, like he expected a cop to jump

out from between the hangers. "Okay," he said. He checked again, then slid the jacket over his shoulders.

Shay swallowed the giddiness that bubbled up inside her. She slipped the second shirt over the first, pulled her bag's strap over the outfit, and walked casually toward the exit. Marco followed a few steps behind.

Just as they reached the hall, someone shouted from inside the store. "Stop! Shoplifters!"

Shay sprang forward, running like the earth was opening behind her, ready to suck her down. The world flashed by in a blur of color. Her heart thumped like a fist against her ribs. A laugh started in her gut and burbled out her lips, the first real laugh she'd uttered in days. The first real feeling since Ryan had left. She was still alive.

Marco caught up with her. "Damn, you're fast," he said, panting.

"You owe me a smoothie," she said, swatting him in the face with a tag.

He caught it and tried to pull her closer. She tugged back, snapping the thin plastic thread. He looked at her like she'd cheated, and she shrugged and skipped toward the escalator feeling light as a bubble just before the pop.

There was no line at the smoothie place, so they went there first.

"I'm getting a strawberry-banana-pineapple with yogurt," Shay said, turning to Marco. "You look like a blueberry-orange guy to me."

"I can be blueberry-orange," he said.

Shay couldn't take the intensity of his stare, so she

scanned the crowds in the food court, her brain allowing itself the dim hope that Ryan was somewhere in the
throng of people.

Kids were sitting on tables, hanging from the trees in
the pots. A gang of what looked like college rejects had
taken over the merry-go-round. Guys in jerseys jumped on
and off the spinning platform, hung from the horses with
one arm. A girl lay on the roof, howling like a wolf.

"It's crazy," Marco said. His breath ruffled her hair, he
was so close.

The darkness crept back in. "Crazy," she whispered.

The mall speaker squealed to life.

"Good morning. I finally have some concrete information for you on the security situation."

A palpable silence fell over the mall.

"It has been determined that we have all been exposed
to a biological agent. It is a form of the flu virus, and I
regret to say that this strain of the virus is unlike any we
have seen before. To prevent contagion from spreading to
the surrounding dense population centers, it has been decided that the mall will be quarantined until such time
as the virus is deemed to have run its course. I will relay
further details as I receive them."

Voices began muttering. Shay looked to Marco. He
stared at a small television behind the smoothie counter.
On its screen was one word: *OUTBREAK*.

A woman screamed. A chair clattered to the ground.
The announcement continued, "If you develop any of the
following symptoms—"

Shay's pulse quickened. More screams, more voices.

The announcement was drowned out by the noise. Shay had to run somewhere, anywhere. A table crashed to the floor. People began to shove past her.

The walls closed in on Shay. She couldn't catch her breath. Marco screamed for her to give him her hand. She looked around. She couldn't see him. There were so many people. A shoulder knocked into her head. She stumbled. Another person shoved her in the back. She fell forward, palms hitting the tiles. She screamed for help. A shoe stabbed her in the back. She tried to crawl for the wall. Someone tripped over her chest, kicking her in the ribs. Tears stung her eyes. She clawed for the safety of the wall.

A shoe connected with her temple.

Everything went dark.

M
A
R
C
O

He couldn't explain what had come over him. All these years of staying off the social radar, of protecting himself, jettisoned for this girl. He was overwhelmed. When Shay touched him, he wanted to cry. He would do anything for her.

But he was so weak. He couldn't hold on to her when she needed him, when real danger struck. When he reached for her, as the crush of people started stampeding toward them, her fingers slipped from his grasp. Why wasn't he bigger, stronger? He could have pushed people aside, lifted her up and to safety. Why, when the crowds barreled down, didn't they trample him instead of her?

After the mob had passed, he found her limp near the window of a leather store. She was unconscious, but still alive. He collapsed with relief, feeling her breath upon his cheek. He had to get her to the medical center. They would know what to do.

He grabbed Shay's hands and dragged her body onto his back. He needed something to help hold her to him. Glancing into the leather store, he saw a messenger bag with a thick strap. Marco snatched it from the rack, slung it over his head, and tucked the bag part under Shay's butt; the strap held her chest to his. Then he began a stumbling shamble down the corridor.

The announcement had transformed the mall. Whereas before, the mall-walkers had seemed dazed and confused, now they were crazed and focused: Every single one of them wanted out. They wanted out of the mall pronto.

People poured out of the stores, pushing against one another as if running a race. Marco could barely keep a straight course as the mob shoved and kicked him out of its way. Forget that he was trying to carry an injured girl. Or that they were all in the exact same cataclysm of crap—a crapaclysm.

Marco lugged Shay onto the escalator. The escalators were jammed full of people, some riding down on the handrail. Suddenly, the machine made an awful shrieking noise. Marco smelled burnt rubber. The escalator slammed to a halt, throwing everyone forward. The ones at the bottom of the steps were shoved to the floor.

People screamed, then began pushing their way down the steps. They were like ants, climbing over one another to get to the bottom of the escalator, as if there were a prize for being the first off. Marco tried to shield Shay from the worst of the violence, but had enough trouble walking her down the steps. One careless woman smacked both Shay and Marco in the face with her giant purse as she stumbled, howling, down the stairs.

In their desperate attempts to reach the exits, people were hanging off the balconies, trying to drop down from one floor to the next. Some climbed down the metal-bracket columns that held the whole mall together. One man missed his footing and free-fell twenty feet, disappearing into the throng below.

Once on the first floor, the people raced for the exits—any exit. Even knowing that the doors were blocked by walls of concrete, they rushed toward them. Crowds formed at the end of each of the first-floor halls. Marco managed to drag Shay's limp body to the head of the PaperClips' hallway, where he saw that the place was packed with screaming, terrified mall-walkers.

"The service hall," Marco muttered, and began slogging back along the main corridor.

Moving against the flow of the masses, Marco saw those left in their wake: an old lady flat on the rug reaching for her purse, a screaming child. He felt that fiery rage explode inside him. Even ants helped their injured. People sucked. *These mall-walkers don't deserve to survive.* But then Shay groaned, and Marco felt how much he wanted to help her, and the rage subsided slightly, if only to make room for the tenderness he felt toward Shay.

Marco opened the service door and collapsed into the silence of the empty hallway. Echoes of the general chaos in the mall vibrated through the walls, but compared to the main corridor, the clean, white service hall was silent as the grave.

Shay slumped on the floor behind him. Marco glanced down the stretch of hallway. He wasn't sure he had the strength to walk himself that far, let alone carry Shay there. But he had to get her help.

Marco hugged Shay's body to him—her arms dragged on the floor as he shifted her torso. With another heaving of strength, Marco managed to get Shay balanced across his spine in a fireman's carry, then put one foot in front of the other down the concrete.

By some miracle, the service door to the PaperClips was still open. Marco stumbled into the stockroom, ready to grab the first doctor he saw. But there was no one there.

The stockroom had been emptied. Two Outsiders stomped through the double doors from the sales floor and began packing the remaining machinery into boxes and loading them onto mobile pallets.

The strap from the satchel snapped and Shay slid from his back to the floor. "Please!" Marco shouted, grabbing the arm of the nearest one. "My friend needs help!"

The Outsider shrugged him off. "Watch the suit!" Then he noticed Shay on the floor. "Sorry, kid," he said. "Orders are to lock down. Anyone not already exposed has to leave. Quarantine."

The guy lugged the last box onto his pallet and pushed the whole thing toward the car-wash doorway of the loading dock.

Marco dragged Shay into the stockroom. One of these assholes had to help.

"Hey!" he shouted as a hazmat suit bustled past. "I need a doctor!"

The person paused, squeezed Marco's shoulder, and said, "I'm sorry. God help us all." Then he ducked out through the loading dock.

Marco stumbled forward, through the stockroom's open doors into the curtained maze of the former sales floor. Overflow patients lay on cots in the halls between the curtains, some unconscious, some aware enough to be screaming for help. The hazmat suits acted like they couldn't see them, stepped over them as if they were trash. The suits were following orders. Some ran boxes through a hole cut in the back wall, others pushed past him toward the Outside. Marco's shouts for help were lost in the chaos. Then one of the curtained walls parted and out stepped the senator.

"Where are my extra stores of Tamiflu?" she yelled at a passing hazmat suit, who pointed to the hole in the wall. She mumbled something into a walkie-talkie, then noticed Marco. "How did you get in here?"

"Service hall," he said, breathless, grateful. "She needs help." He lifted Shay off his back and laid her down across a chair.

The senator gave them a pitying look, then bent her head to the side as if cracking her neck. She touched Shay's forehead. Shay's eyelids fluttered and she moaned. The senator pointed to a plastic crate. "Use one of the cold packs in there and wrap it to wherever you feel a bump on her head." Then she bustled off into the stockroom.

Marco did as he was told—his brain was too scared to try to rustle up its own thoughts. He poked through the plastic crate until he found a white bag that said "Instant Cold Pack." He followed the directions—cracked it, shook it—and felt it become freezing cold against his palms. The sensation brought tears to his eyes. Something that worked as it was supposed to!

He touched Shay's beautiful head and felt a goose egg above and behind her right temple. He pressed the cold pack to her, and she groaned in response.

Marco then became aware of a sound like thunder coming from the front of the store. No, not thunder. Banging. The crowds were banging on the plywood wall that covered the PaperClips. They were going to bust through and storm the medical ward. The two of them would be crushed if they didn't get out of the way.

Marco grabbed a roll of gauze, wrapped the ice pack to Shay's forehead, and lifted her off the chair.

The banging was now mixed with horrible creaking sounds—the wood was giving way. The cries of the sick became screams as some of the rioters broke through the plywood door and came raging into the curtain maze. Marco dragged Shay as fast as he could, waiting for the ominous sound of breaking glass. That was the signal for when the true chaos would erupt. A security guard with a megaphone began shouting for people to remain calm. The screams only got louder.

Marco stumbled into the stockroom. The senator stood in front of the loading dock, the overhead door of which was closed. Every few seconds, the metal rattled—the Outsiders were sealing them in.

The service hallway was only feet away. Marco hefted Shay's body and stumbled forward, nearly butting heads with a guard.

"Senator!" the guard shouted. "We have to seal this door!"

The senator stared for a heartbeat longer at the loading dock doorway, then she turned, bumping into Marco. It took her a moment to realize that he was a person and not some empty box, but then she lifted Shay's other arm and helped Marco carry her into the service corridor. Just as they crossed the threshold, Marco heard the glass of the front windows of the PaperClips smash.

The cop pulled the double doors closed behind them and locked the handles with a crowbar. Marco heard the rising cacophony of shouts from inside the PaperClips. The senator left Shay in Marco's arms and began walking down the hallway, away from the mob.

"You're just going to let this happen?" Marco asked, incredulous.

The senator turned, a sad look on her face. "What would you like me to do?" she asked. "Please, tell me, what am I supposed to do?"

Marco had no words. The leader of this mall was asking him what to do. *Him*, Marco Carvajal: a nobody, a busboy, a kid.

The senator shrugged, sighing, then turned away again and disappeared down the hallway.

Marco slumped against the wall and slid down, holding Shay to him. Someone banged against the barred service doors and he jumped, sure the end was coming for them all. But the bar held. For the moment, they were safe.

Marco hugged Shay and waited for it all to be over.

L E X I

exi lifted Maddie's head and dribbled some water
into her mouth. She sputtered, then swallowed. Lexi
pulled the face mask back over Maddie's mouth.

"I don't know why you're doing this," Maddie said, lying back onto her pillow of sweaters. "But thanks."

"You'd do the same for me," Lexi said, rubbing sanitizer over her hands and face. Her skin stung from the
endless applications.

"I wouldn't," Maddie said. "Isn't that horrible?" She
coughed into the mask.

Lexi stood, using the nearby shelf for support. "Yes,
that is horrible."

Maddie grabbed Lexi's ankle. "I'm sorry I was such a
bitch the other day, making you do that lap dance and
everything." Her blue eyes were ringed in purple and
her hair was plastered against her forehead from having
sweated so horribly after her fever broke.

Lexi shook off her fingers and smiled. "Yeah, well, now you have all the time in the world to make it up to me." They'd heard the announcement earlier that morning about the quarantine.

Maddie's eyes smiled. "I guess I do."

When Lexi had arrived yesterday, she'd found six people lying in various states of illness around the floor of the Abercrombie. A salesperson, who was feeling chilled and achy herself, offered to help Lexi and move them all into the stockroom in the back if Lexi shared her medicine. Lexi had gratefully agreed.

It had been a long, horrible, scary night. First thing Lexi did was put face masks on them all; even she wore one, though she knew it wouldn't do anything. The saleslady soon succumbed to the flu and had to be cared for like the others. Lexi poured swallows of soup down each person's throat and dosed them all with Tylenol and vitamins. When they felt too hot, she covered their foreheads with the ice packs. She helped them hobble to the tiny staff bathroom when they needed it. So far, everyone but the saleslady's fever had broken.

When the announcement was made and the screaming started, Lexi locked the stockroom door and barred the doors to the service hall. She did not want the riot to come to them. Now the screams sounded farther away. But there was still screaming.

"Lexi!"

She had to wait for the person to yell a second time before she believed it.

"Dad?" she asked.

She ran to the stockroom door and flicked open the

lock. Her father was poking into the racks of clothes.

"Dad!" she yelled, feeling a rush of relief.

He turned and grabbed her, hugging her tight to him. "Thank god," he whispered into her hair. "Ginger said you would be here, and I prayed she was right. I have to get you out of here."

In the store, the screaming from the mall was louder. "And go where?" Lexi asked. "Stay with me," she said. "It's safe in the stockroom."

Her father held her shoulders and looked her in the face. "It is not safe in the stockroom," he said. "It's not safe anywhere but the Apple Store. The police can protect us there."

Lexi pulled away from him. "I can't leave," she said. "There are people who need me here."

Her father looked at her like he did not know her. "Lex, please." He took her hand. "Can't you listen to me just this once?"

A tear tickled her cheek. "Please stay and help me."

Dad started to cry too. He nodded. She led him into the stockroom.

They began changing the sick people, Arthur, the boys, and Lexi, the girls. They needed to get them out of their sweat-ridden, germy clothes before they got chilled. Four of the kids were feeling well enough that they could change themselves. Lexi and her dad just handed them whatever clothes were within arm's reach and a wet cloth.

"Here," Lexi said, dropping a long-sleeved tee and a pair of sweats onto Maddie's winter-coat blanket.

Maddie raised an eyebrow at the offering. "This doesn't even match."

"All complaints can be directed to the Department of I Don't Give a Crap."

Maddie snorted a laugh that morphed into a fit of coughing. "You're literally—*cough*—killing me."

Lexi walked around the shelf to where she'd left the saleslady. The woman had her face buried in a stack of sweatshirts.

"Don't cough on them," Lexi said, putting a hand on the woman's shoulder. "We might need th—"

The saleslady rolled toward Lexi. Her eyes were open. Glassy. Dead.

It wasn't until her father pulled her away from the body that Lexi realized she was screaming. Dad sat her in a different aisle, then went back to the woman. Lexi sat, stunned, trembling.

"I thought she was getting better," Lexi mumbled when her father returned. "I swear, I thought her fever would break, like the others."

Her father wiped her skin with sanitizer. "There is nothing you could have done to save her," he said. "We should get all these kids down to the med center." He squeezed her hands. "You don't have to do this alone."

Lexi fell forward, hugging him, and let herself cry.

Her father ordered her to put on some clean clothes before they moved anyone out of the Abercrombie. Lexi went out into the store, more to clear her head than because she wanted to browse the displays. She found some new jeans, a T-shirt, and hoodie and changed in a dark corner. Deciding she could use some new shoes, she headed back toward the stockroom to see what they had in her size.

"Hey!" a voice shouted. "Hand over the register key!"

Lexi turned, surprised by the bizarre request, and found herself face-to-face with a wiry dude wielding what looked like a drill.

Are you kidding me?

"I don't work here," she said, frozen. "I don't have a key."

The guy squeezed the drill and there was a bang and something whizzed past Lexi. "Get me the freaking key!"

The guy's face suddenly changed. "I thought you were alone." He bolted out of the store.

Lexi turned. Her father stood in the doorway of the stockroom. Red soaked through his shirt near his right shoulder. He stumbled forward.

Lexi ran to him. "Nononononono," she muttered, catching him as he sagged into her embrace.

Her father touched his shoulder, teeth gritted. "I think it hit bone," he said.

"What do I do?" Lexi said.

"Get me to the PaperClips," her father said.

He tried to push himself up. Lexi shoved her shoulder under his left arm. They lurched out of the Abercrombie.

The hall on the second floor was nearly empty, but from the top of the motionless escalator, Lexi saw the crowds—a sea of people—raging beneath her. Her father tried to hold his own weight on the railing with his right arm and red bled out across his shirt.

"Just lean on me," Lexi said.

They hobbled, one step at a time, down the escalator. As they neared the bottom, some kid shoved past Arthur, screaming, "Move it, Grandpa!"

Arthur was thrown forward. Lexi lost her grip on his arm. Her father yelped, fell off the step, then tried to catch himself on the railing.

He screamed. Lexi screamed. She dove forward, trying to throw her body beneath him before he fell, but she was too slow. He landed against the stone of the first-floor hall.

"Dad!" she said, kneeling beside him.

He groaned. "I think I broke the arm," he said, "catching myself."

Lexi heard feet on the escalator. Her father would be trampled if she didn't move him.

"We have to get away from here," she said.

Her father nodded. He rolled himself over by throwing his hips. His left arm hung at an odd angle.

Lexi pressed her back to her father's, then pushed against him with her legs, lifting him off the ground. He stumbled forward, grabbed the railing with his right arm, shouted obscenities, and stood on his own.

"Let's go," he whispered.

Lexi nodded.

Her father lifted his right arm and Lexi gently pushed against his rib cage, trying to keep from touching the shoulder.

In the short hall leading to the PaperClips, an enormous number of people were amassed against the exit doors.

"There's no way we're getting through that," she said to her dad.

He watched for a second. "No, this is good." He drove himself in between the first few people, then looked back at her, wincing. "See? They can hold me up."

Lexi shoved into the crowd after him and they moved slowly through the undulating bodies, being tossed one way, then another, at times being lifted off their feet entirely. It was like swimming, only unpleasant and loud and terrifying. Lexi felt the hot mist of people's breath on her skin like a poison. She tried to hold her breath, but that only made her feel sick. Her father pushed forward, every once in a while barking with pain as someone hit his shoulder or arm. Somehow, after an eternity, they pressed against the plywood of the PaperClips' barrier.

They slipped along the outside of the crowd against the wall to the door. Lexi had to throw herself back into the throng to eke open the door, but somehow they both managed to jam themselves into the empty space behind the plywood. The door was slammed shut behind them. Dad tumbled to the floor.

Lexi shouted for help, but with all the screaming and shouting, who could hear her?

"I'll run in and get someone," she said. Her father nodded.

The people began banging on the plywood wall. The beams groaned.

"Hurry," he said.

Inside, Lexi saw only people on gurneys. Coughing, screaming, prostrate patients, but no doctors. She yelled for help, flapping open each curtain as she ducked through the maze of rooms. But there was no one.

The wood groaned louder. Snapped.

Dad.

Lexi bolted back toward the entrance. He'd be crushed. She had to save him.

The wall collapsed, crashed into the glass entryway of the PaperClips. Lexi turned from the spray of shards, throwing her arm over her face, and crouched behind a gurney. Then the gurney was on top of her. She screamed with pain—the bed had fallen across her legs just above her knees, tossing the patient who'd been in it onto her back. A wall of curtain fell on top of the pile. Feet trampled the fabric around her, but the bulk of the gurney must have worked to drive the masses of people aside.

She wiggled her toes—her legs must not have been broken. She curled her head down and wrapped her arms over her skull and neck. The person on top of her coughed; luckily, the body lay perpendicular to her over her butt, the head several feet from her rear.

The feet pounded. Voices screamed. Glass crashed to the floor. More shouting. More crashing. Then less. Fewer voices. Then only the cries and groans of the other people buried in the wreckage.

Lexi strained against the weight of the gurney. She could not move. She screamed for help. The only answer was the hacking cough of the dying patient on top of her.

RYAN

Ryan pulled the thick jacket tighter around his shoulders. The shivers were overwhelming now, rattling his teeth if he unclenched his jaws. He was cold, so very cold, and couldn't get warm no matter how many jackets he buried himself under.

They'd hidden in Harry's after escaping the jail in the parking garage. Mr. Reynolds had thought they could hole up in one of the back sections between the crowded racks and avoid the cops. He'd been right—not a soul had bothered them. Ryan had excused himself, saying he'd hurt his shoulder tackling the guard, and curled up in the winter coats. He wasn't sure how many hours had passed—he'd fallen in and out of consciousness. Once, he'd opened his eyes to darkness, a spinning black that terrified him like he was a kid again. Cracking open his eyelids now, he saw the comforting glare of the overhead lighting. It seemed unsteady, but swirling light was somehow better than swirling black.

"Ryan?"

The voice was nearby, though it sounded muffled to Ryan's ears. A hand shook his shoulder.

"Shrimp." Mike peeled back the jacket. His eyes bulged.

It must have been bad. Were his fingers blue? His eyes red? When would the coughing start? How long until he died?

Mr. Reynolds stood a good distance apart. "We should leave him," he said. "No way he's going to make an escape in that condition."

"We don't leave a man behind," Drew said from somewhere behind Ryan. "I'll carry him."

Mike tucked the jacket tighter around Ryan's shoulders. "He's too sick." Mike stood. Ryan wanted to plead with them not to leave him, that he could walk, but his brain had lost contact with his mouth. He groaned. It was the best he could do.

"We have to get him some food, medicine." Mike wiped his hands on a T-shirt hanging from the nearest rack.

Mr. Reynolds stepped closer. "We have to get out of here."

Mike stood. "This isn't a negotiation."

"Don't mess with me, kid. I'm not blowing our escape just to save your pal."

"Let me say it again." Mike pulled a gun from his waistband. "This isn't a negotiation."

Mr. Reynolds backed away. "Where'd you get that?"

"The cop." Mike held the gun level with Mr. Reynolds's chest.

"Dude," Drew muttered.

Mr. Reynolds put up his hands. "Fine," he said. "We'll get him some food."

Mike lowered the gun. "Glad we agree."

Sometime later, Mike woke Ryan again. "We have to move," he whispered, handing Ryan a bottle of Sportade.

Ryan nodded. He sipped the liquid, which even at room temperature felt cold. Everything was cold. He slid his arms into the sleeves of the jacket. Mike zipped the front, then pulled him to standing. As Mike helped Ryan hobble down the aisle, he explained that an announcement had been made that the government was quarantining the mall because of some flu and that people had gone insane as a result.

"I have it," Ryan said.

"Duh." Mike smiled and gave him a light noogie. "But that doesn't mean we're not getting your sick ass out of here."

Ryan could almost forget how terrifying Mike had looked holding that gun.

The plan was to go to the HomeMart and get a jackhammer and blast through an exterior wall. Mr. Reynolds hoped to break through after nightfall and then crawl through the shadows to safety.

The four took the escalator up to the second floor—the rioters crowded the first level.

"None of these sheep are getting out the main exits,"

Mr. Reynolds said, smiling that thin smile of his. "But we have to thank them for all the noise. The cops couldn't hear a jackhammer if it was drilling directly into their skulls."

The second floor was not entirely empty. Individuals and small gangs raided the abandoned stores, dragging loot out in piles. The four had to swerve around the looters and their troves.

Ryan tried to keep pace with the others, shambling along on feet that felt like they weighed fifty pounds each. Mike barked encouragement into his ear—You keep moving, step by step, Shrimp. You get to that goal. Ryan stepped over and over for Mike. But then his foot caught on something and the walls shifted and he was on the ground.

"Get him up!" Mr. Reynolds shouted.

The world spun again. Blurs of color swirled in front of him. Mike and Drew hefted him up.

"In here," Mike growled, dragging Ryan backward out of the hall.

From the posters, Ryan knew they were in Shep's. He liked that he would die in Shep's. Maybe Mike could hold him against the climbing wall one last time. Mike sat Ryan on a weight bench and turned to tell Drew something. Ryan thought he saw a man in the back of the store.

Then Mr. Reynolds was screaming. A red-fletched hunting arrow stuck out from his shoe.

A voice came from the back of the store. "I've taken over Shep's," the man yelled. "Go find your own place."

Mike dragged Ryan behind a display, then Mr. Reynolds collapsed on the floor beside them and stared at his foot, whimpering. Drew stood at the edge of the display eyeing their attacker.

"One guy," he said to Mike. "Back left corner. Compound bow. That's it."

Mike stood. He glared through a hole in the display wall at the guy. "I am sick of being screwed with." He nudged Drew in the shoulder. "You distract him over by the kayaks."

Drew nodded and skulked to the end of the aisle.

Mike grabbed Mr. Reynolds's hand, which was on the arrow's shaft. "Don't pull it out." Then Mike handed Ryan the Sportade. "Drink."

Drew bounded along the side wall, ducking from display to display. Mike sprinted across the center of the store to the opposite wall. Ryan crawled to the edge of the display to watch.

Drew dove for the kayaks, knocking several over. The guy fired an arrow into the hull of the one closest to Drew. Mike appeared from behind the display nearest the guy and shot him point blank in the temple. The man fell forward across the counter. Red spatter marred the wall.

Ryan felt even colder. Not sick cold, but like he might never be able to not see that red stain. He dragged himself back behind the display. He wished he hadn't moved.

"Serves the bastard right," Mr. Reynolds said, gently prodding at his shoe.

Shadows appeared at the edges of Ryan's vision. They were coming for him, the demons. He was dying and he had just witnessed a murder and he had maybe killed two cops himself and these shadows were coming now for him. He didn't want to die. He waved his hands, tried to push the shadows away.

Something grabbed his arm. The shadows were everywhere now. He begged them to leave him alone. He didn't want to die.

The black took over and everything was cold.

DAY

SEVEN

·FRIDAY·

S
H
A
Y

She woke with a start in the darkness, heart racing.
A body pressed against her side—was she under
some pile? She remembered a wave of people
screaming as they rushed toward her.

Her eyes adjusted and she saw the red lettering of an
exit sign far down the hall. So she was not stuck under
a pile of bodies. She was in some hallway. Her breathing
slowed.

She guessed that the body next to her was Marco's—at
least, she hoped that was true. She shuffled out from under him. He shifted in his sleep and readjusted against the
wall, but did not wake.

Shay's purse was still slung around her body. She
fished inside the bag and took out her keys—one of them
had a tiny LED light on it. Her father had given it to her as
a safety measure. "In case you're ever trying to get home
in the dark," he'd said, pressing the bulky red key into

her hand. Remembering his words brought tears to her eyes. *I'm trying to get home, Bapuji.* All she wanted was to be home.

Given the almost total darkness of the hallway, her tiny lamp illuminated the walls with what seemed like a brilliant white light. The sleeper was indeed Marco. He sat slumped in a corner at the end of a long, white hallway. Shay flashed the light to her left and saw two large doors, one of which had "PaperClips" printed in block type on it.

They were in the service hallway outside the medical center. Marco must have dragged her down here from the food court. She touched her fingers to her temple, remembering suddenly being knocked over and blacking out. A loose band of gauze was wrapped around her head. She winced at the size of the goose egg under the skin above her right ear. Her head throbbed, but the darkness kept the pain from feeling too bad.

Why, though, were they in the hallway and not in the actual medical ward? Worry oozed through her belly. Had the stampede that ran over her in the food court spread throughout the mall?

Preeti.

The doors to the PaperClips were barred on the service hallway side by a crowbar. Shay stood and pulled the rod of metal from between the handles.

The stockroom was as dark as the service hallway. Shining her small light in front of her, Shay saw smashed boxes, cases of pens dumped across the floor, broken plastic and glass. She walked carefully toward where the loading dock should have been—where she'd guessed the hazmat people had their passage to the real world.

The door was closed—not a ray of light pierced the black. It must have been walled over like the exits.

The medical teams had left, sealed them in. But what about all the patients? Had they taken Preeti and Nani with them? *Please* . . .

Shay navigated through the debris on the stockroom floor to the doors that led into the main part of the store. What had once been the emergency medical center was a disaster zone.

The maze of curtains had collapsed, creating tents in some places; while in other areas, the fabric was shredded, tangled amidst the rods of the metal frames that had held the curtains up. The glass of the front wall to the PaperClips was completely smashed and beyond that, the plywood barrier lay in pieces against the wall in the corridor.

Something groaned off to Shay's left. Lifting a piece of curtain-wall still in its frame, Shay found a woman lying on the floor beside a toppled gurney.

The medical teams had left the patients. Had left them here to be crushed.

"Preeti!" she screamed.

"Help!" a voice cried. Then another. Violent coughs erupted from beneath a pile near the wall. Shay began digging through the mess. Hot tears ran down her face. *I'm coming, Preeti* . . . Her head throbbed. The piles of wreckage moved as bodies writhed beneath them. Shay stepped into a clear patch of ground. A bluish hand shot out and grabbed her ankle. Shay kicked the hand off. She had to find Preeti. She lifted a wall of fabric and found a person in a hazmat suit curled over a toppled bed.

Shay touched the suit. The person started, rolled over.

"Is it over?" the person asked. He wasn't wearing a face mask.

"Shouldn't you be outside with the rest of them?" Shay said, voice dripping with venom.

The man stood. "My suit was torn in the evacuation. I was deemed exposed and had to stay behind."

Shay recognized him from earlier with Nani—*Dr. Chen.* "Have you seen my sister?"

He shook his head. "She should be where you left her." He scanned the disaster zone. "What have we done?" He sounded humbled.

Good. Shay pushed past him and began digging through the junk once again. He worked next to her, helped her lift the heavy pieces. He paused to check the people they found; Shay kept going.

Lifting a panel of curtain, Shay found her.

"Dr. Chen!" she screamed.

Preeti was beside her gurney, which lay on its side. She wasn't moving. *Why isn't she moving?*

Dr. Chen took Shay's arm and held her steady. "Let me take a look."

The whole world was blurry. Shay rubbed her fist across her eyes. Her contacts were so dry.

"She's asleep," Dr. Chen said from somewhere below. "Her fever has broken. She's going to be okay."

Shay dropped to her knees and hugged Dr. Chen. He patted her back awkwardly, like he was not used to comforting. As Shay remembered, his bedside manner had been nonexistent.

They righted Preeti's gurney and Dr. Chen laid her on the mattress. Shay took off one of her T-shirts and dabbed Preeti's sweaty face.

Her eyes fluttered. "Is it morning?" she asked. She must have slept through the riots. Preeti had all the luck.

"You're better," Shay said, her words choked by a sob.

Preeti smiled, then curled her knees up. "Tired," she said.

Shay kissed her forehead.

"Where's Nani?" Preeti mumbled.

Nani.

Shay tugged on Dr. Chen's shoulder. He helped a man back onto his cot, then turned to Shay. "Glad to see your sister made it," he said.

"Where's the ICU?" she asked.

Dr. Chen seemed surprised she knew about it. "I'm not sure it's safe to go back there."

"Just tell me where it is."

He led her to the back corner of the sales floor, opposite the windows. As they walked, Shay noticed a high-pitched whine that grew louder. A hole had been cut in the wall leading into the neighboring store. Thick plastic hung where a door should have been.

"We needed to keep the facility separate," Dr. Chen said, pushing aside the doorway.

The whine became a shriek and it was coming from the machines: the sound of flatlining. Shay covered her ears. There were rows of patients, all with tubes in their mouths like Nani. Shay couldn't tell which machines were making the noise.

Shay ran to the closest one. An old man. His machine wailed. Air pumped into him, but his chest didn't move. He was dead, his body cold.

Shay checked the next bed. Another corpse. And another. And another. Nani wasn't like them. She was alive. The faces were blue-black. Each suck of air from the machines forced a froth of blood up the tubes. Nani couldn't be like them.

One of the blue faces was familiar. No. She was asleep. Not dead. Sleeping.

Dr. Chen grabbed Shay's shoulders. "You shouldn't have to see this."

Shay wanted to scream. But she was cold, frozen. Her eyes burned, dry as paper.

"Is she dead?"

Dr. Chen wrapped his arm around her, pulled her away. "Let's get you back to your sister."

Her legs gave way first, stumbling out from under her. The room went black. She felt Dr. Chen grab her, keep her from hitting the floor. But all she heard was the shrieking of the machines, the screams of the dead.

RYAN

ight shone red through Ryan's eyelids. He was alive.
He opened his eyes slowly. His lips felt dry and cracked.

"He's awake," Mr. Reynolds said from off to Ryan's right.

Ryan tried to move his arms, but found them pinned to his chest by the sleeping bag he was packed in. He pushed up onto his elbows. Mike knelt at his side and looked like he might cry.

"I knew you'd make it," he said, though for Mike to be near tears, Ryan feared his survival had seemed a long shot at some point in the night.

Drew came over with something that smelled like chicken soup. "From the employees' locker," he said. "Cup o' crap." He spooned some into Ryan's mouth.

Ryan sputtered at the hot liquid. "I think I can feed myself," he said.

Drew feigned offense. "Oh, look who's the big man now."

Taking the hot cup in his hands, Ryan wondered at the gift of this morning. He was alive.

"Now can we get out of here?" Mr. Reynolds said, glancing out Shep's entrance. "Of course, it's too quiet to drill." He picked up a tennis ball and chucked it at the wall. The bong of the ball against the paint seemed to echo throughout the post-riot silence.

They'd lost their chance of escape via jackhammer because of him. But Ryan couldn't feel guilty. He hadn't choked on his own blood, his fingers were still pinkish white—he was alive. The morning sunlight fought its way through a thin layer of clouds to shine on the tile in the hall. How long since he'd really appreciated the sky?

The skylights.

He slurped a steaming mouthful from the cup. "I know a way out," he said.

It didn't take long to get the guys into harnesses—companies made them practically idiot-proof at this point. Ryan pulled two lengths of rope from the rack and collected a bunch of quickdraws and regular carabiners, and a belay device.

The plan was for Ryan to free-climb the column closest to the central skylight. The columns, which stretched from the first floor all the way to the ceiling, were essentially colorfully painted scaffolding. Four thick poles formed a square, between which diagonally placed metal beams formed irregular triangles. Every few yards, there was a neon sign or artsy metal thing strapped to the poles. But up by the ceiling, the scaffold was clear.

Once at the top, Ryan would belay the others as they climbed. When all three reached the ceiling, they would use an ice ax to bust open the skylight and escape onto the roof.

The only problem was that Ryan still felt like crap. The soup and two bottles of Sportade helped, but they only went so far. He'd washed the fever-sweat from his body in the little staff bathroom in the back and changed into some climbing shorts and a T-shirt. In one of the bathroom closets, he'd found some Tylenol and pounded two. He felt a little better, but not one hundred percent.

Ryan hung the ropes from his harness and tied on his climbing shoes. The others hovered nearby. They'd all judged his plan to be a winner. "That's QB thinking," Drew had said. Mike had merely clapped him on the shoulder like a proud father. Mr. Reynolds had begrudgingly agreed to the plan after bitching about having to engage in physical activity. Mike had told him he was free to stay behind.

They walked cautiously up to the third floor. The halls were oddly empty, like the riot had cleared all the people from the mall. But every once in a while they heard coughing or crying, betraying the people still camped out in the stores.

Ryan planned to climb without a safety rope, but when Mike stood at the base of the column and took in the height of the climb that remained coupled with the drop to the first floor courtyard, he'd strapped on the belay device and asked Ryan what to do.

"No way I'm letting you die after saving your ass all this time," Mike said, smirking.

Ryan showed him the basics of belaying a person—there wasn't much to show and Mike was a fast learner. When he finished, he took Mike's hand.

"I owe you," he said, pulling Mike in for a shoulder bump. Funny how a guy could completely freak you out, but also be the only person you trusted.

Mike patted Ryan's arm, almost hugging him. "Thad's always had my back, and I will always have yours."

The first few feet were easy, but once Ryan got halfway to the ceiling, his hands began to sweat from nerves. Patting chalk powder from his pouch onto his palms, he tried to think of anything but the plash of the central fountain some forty feet below. He fastened a 'biner to the scaffold around his belay rope—at least he'd only fall so far.

The last time he climbed, he'd been with Shay. He wondered where she was, why she hadn't met him in the parking garage, though now he was grateful that she hadn't. He didn't want her to know about the cops he'd bulldozed.

Thinking about the cops didn't help his sweat problem.

So he thought of Shay falling toward him, the way the harness had wrapped around her waist, the smoothness of her skin when he'd touched her.

And he was at the top. With a hard-on. But at the top. Sixty feet stretched between him and the first floor, but he was mere inches from the skylight and freedom. He pressed his fingers to the cold glass, then clipped himself to the column with a quickdraw. He arranged the rope through the bottom carabiners of two other quickdraws, attached to two points on the scaffold, and signaled Mike to release the belay device. Ryan pulled it up, hooked the belay device to his harness, and threaded the other end of the rope back down to Mike.

Mr. Reynolds climbed next. The fact that he was old and out of shape combined with his bum foot made him doubly slow. The wait was agonizing. Ryan sucked water from the pouch he'd strapped to his back to keep the tickles in his throat at bay.

Once Mr. Reynolds was up, Ryan hooked him to the column with a quickdraw, then lowered the rope down for Mike to climb. Mike was fast, scampering up the rungs like a squirrel on a tree.

A hand pulled the ice ax from the webbing of Ryan's hydration pack. Ryan glanced over his shoulder, securing the belay rope tight across his thigh. Mr. Reynolds had shuffled to the side of the column nearest the skylight. He had the ax poised below the glass.

"What are you doing?" Ryan yelled. "The plan is to wait for everyone to get to the top before busting out."

"I've waited long enough."

Mr. Reynolds smashed the skylight. Ryan threw his free arm over his face as splinters of glass rained down into the fountain below. Screams erupted from the first floor— apparently, they had attracted an audience.

Mr. Reynolds hoisted himself through the hole in the glass. Fresh air tousled Ryan's hair. He'd forgotten the scent of fall air, the feeling of crispness.

Mike pulled himself to the top. "What the hell?" he shouted.

Ryan heard the pulsing chop of a helicopter's blades through the broken window. As it grew louder, a breeze gusted to match the noise.

Mike pulled himself up and peered through the hole. "We're screwed." He dropped back down.

Ryan heard tromping footsteps. He could almost see the cops on the roof. Mr. Reynolds would be driven back through the hole. Ryan unhooked the 'biner from Mike's harness and attached it to the back of his own. He handed Mike the belay device.

"Catch me," he said.

Just then, Mr. Reynolds plummeted through the fractured glass, dropping down toward the fountain, screaming.

Ryan pushed off from the column and fell. Adrenaline rushed through his veins. He opened his arms and legs in time to wrap them around Mr. Reynolds. Mike pulled the line taut. Between the gut-busting force of the rope catching and the drag of Mr. Reynolds's body, Ryan nearly lost his grip, but the bear hug held them together.

The line swung toward the strips of walkway spanning the open courtyard. When the line bent and swung them under the third-floor passage, Ryan released Mr. Reynolds onto the second-floor walkway. The old bastard dropped onto the tile and cried out.

Ryan owed him nothing now.

The rope swung back out into the void and Ryan closed his eyes. Blood pumped through him. Sweat dripped off his face. He was alive.

Opening his eyes, he saw a crowd of cops gathering. They were screwed, all of them. Nowhere to hide dangling in space. But he was alive. For the moment, that was enough.

M
A
R
C
O

His first thought upon waking: Where is Shay? Her body had been beside him, now he was alone. The lights buzzed overhead. He heard voices from inside the PaperClips.

On the sales floor, a man in a hazmat suit stood knee-deep in toppled curtains and equipment. His tent of a helmet hung behind him—an Outsider now trapped on the inside. The senator was in the room with him, as were a couple of security guards and a cop. They were all digging through the trash. The voices came from beneath the trash.

"Where's Shaila?" Marco yelled.

The hazmat guy pointed to a part of the room behind him, the already cleared part. Marco found her asleep on a gurney beside the little sister. The grandmother was nowhere in sight. From how sick she'd been, she was most likely dead. Shay and the sister were alone in this mall. Like him.

Marco touched Shay's arm. She rolled slightly, groaned. His mind whirred into action. They needed food, a safe place to hide out, medicine. He could try to steal supplies from the EMC, but the cops would be on him before he got halfway out the door. Did he dare venture out into the chaos of the mall proper alone?

Two guards made their way back toward Marco—it was the guys from the restaurant the other day. Marco hid behind a curtain that had been righted and turned on his pilfered police radio.

"We have one on the third floor, and another is descending the pillar. You guys grab the kid hanging from the rope."

"And you're sure it's the demolition derby guys?"

"Yep—the ID on the guy at the bottom of the pillar says Drew Bonner. No doubt it's Richter on the pole and Murphy on the rope. Old guy's being subdued on a second-floor walkway."

So Richter had been the one to organize the escape through the garage. He should have stuck with Marco. Now he was one descent away from being arrested.

And then it dawned on him: He could help Mike Richter. And Richter could watch his back and protect Shay and the sister. It was a match made in hell.

Marco stuck the radio into his jacket. He tucked the thin hospital blanket around Shay and the sister, then left through the back doors into the service hallway. He slid the cop's card key through the elevator's reader and the doors opened.

I am the master of all I survey . . .

He rode up to the third floor, then exited the service halls into the main corridor. Scanning the area, he spotted Richter on the central column nearest the movie theaters. Two cops stood at the base, one with a hand on Drew Bonner's arm, both of which were behind his back, most likely in cuffs. A few people gawked from inside the entrance to the movie theater, but it was early yet, so the halls were empty.

Based on the distribution of service doors near the Grill'n'Shake, Marco assumed that a service door existed down the hall away from the theaters. *But how to distract the cops?* There was no time to search for the perfect tool; he glanced around him.

A fire extinguisher.

Marco ripped the thing from the wall. An alarm began to sound. The cops started, looked around. Marco walked straight up to them and sprayed the two in the face. A cloud of white exploded from the extinguisher. The two cops fell to the floor, coughing and wheezing and holding their throats.

Drew began to cough—a bonus for Marco. "It's the goddamed mallrat!" he shouted up to Mike.

Marco blasted the cops again. "I'm your knight in shining armor, you ass."

Mike hopped off the column. He unhooked himself from the rope. "What's your plan, Taco?" he said.

Marco blasted the cops again; they fell back. "Follow me."

He dropped the fire extinguisher and bolted for the service hallway. Mike and Drew raced after him. At the door, Marco slid the key through the port. The scanner flashed green and the door opened with a clank—the magnetic lock unlocking. He pulled it open.

"After you," he said.

Mike and Drew dashed in and Marco closed the door behind all three of them.

"We have to get Ryan," Mike growled.

"Follow me," Marco said, leading them down the hall. There had to be an elevator somewhere.

Drew strode up to his side. "I thought your card key only worked on the door near the Grease'n'Suck?"

"I got a new key."

At the elevator, Marco slid the card through and the doors opened. "Again, after you," he said.

They trundled into the elevator and Marco slid the card key through the panel and selected the first floor.

Mike pulled a six-inch hunting knife from his waistband and sliced through the plastic cuffs on Bonner's wrists. Then they turned on Marco.

"We appreciate the rescue," Mike said. Using the butt of the knife, he lifted his shirt to reveal a gun in his waistband. "Not that I needed it. But I'm a little confused as to your motives."

"I want protection," Marco said, trying to ignore the gun's presence. "We're trapped in here for potentially the rest of our lives. I want to know you have my back." Marco slipped the card into his pocket. "And there's a girl and her sister. I need to know you'll watch out for all three of us."

"What's to keep me from gutting you and taking your new card?"

Marco was surprised only by the up-front nature of Mike's threat. He pulled out two cards. "Only I know which is mine and which is the universal," he said. "And I will snap them both in half before I die, I promise you." Mike and Drew took a less menacing posture. "Plus, I know these back hallways. It will take you days to discover what I already know."

Marco could almost hear the wheels spinning in Mike's brain. They were not so dissimilar, he realized.

"All right," Mike said, holding out his hand.

Marco did not take the hand. "Let's not pretend we're anything more than allies of circumstance."

Mike smiled. "I'm beginning to take a liking to you, Taco."

"I won't let it go to my head."

The doors opened. Marco stepped out. "If you run, you can use the fire extinguisher at the end of the hall to free Ryan. Two cops are waiting for him near the fountain."

Drew loped for the extinguisher.

Mike stayed behind. "Come with us," he said.

"What's in it for me?" Marco had his hand in his pants pocket, his exit card at the ready—he'd notched the edge of the universal card near the corner to identify it.

Mike smiled. "The mall is our oyster," he said. "Between the two of us, I think we can make all our dreams come true."

Marco took his hand off the card. He pulled the police radio from his jacket and turned it on.

Mike's face expressed approval. "You've been busy."

Marco couldn't help but smile at Mike's praise. He

turned the radio off. "They almost have Ryan down off the rope. We'd better move."

They caught up with Drew near the door, then busted out, extinguisher blasting. People ran from their path, screaming. They were the masters of all they surveyed.

L
E
X
I

From beneath the pile of wreckage that was once the medical center, Lexi could hear people around her, voices talking. That was all she could sense beyond the darkness. Fabric pressed against her face, making it hard to breathe. She angled her head, creating a larger pocket of air between the curtain and the floor.

Every few seconds, she cried out to the people, banged on the curtain above her. She couldn't feel her feet anymore. The person on top of her had stopped coughing. The body felt cold against her skin. She would not die like this.

It took the voices time (minutes? hours?) to get close to her. She saw the bright flash of Lights On and that brought some hope. Soon, she could hear actual words, then the curtain was lifted off her.

The man's eyes widened upon finding her. "I've got a

live one!" he shouted, then knelt and pushed the gurney off of her.

Pins and needles pricked through Lexi's legs as the blood flowed back through them. She cried out—it was so painful, she wished he'd just left the bed on top of her.

"Lexi!" Her mother pushed past a stack of crates and fell beside her, began to kiss her face.

Lexi dragged her legs from under the body and threw her arms around her mother's neck. The pins and needles were agonizing, like a million bees stinging her from the inside. "Did you get Dad?" she asked, pulling back to arrange her body better.

Dotty sat straighter. "He's in here?"

Lexi explained how Arthur had been near the plywood wall when the rioters broke through. The Senator immediately ran toward the broken front wall of the store. The man who'd found Lexi—Dr. Chen, she was told—joined the Senator.

Lexi crawled from behind the gurney to better see where they were digging. "He was closer to the center, near the door!" she shouted.

Soon, they lifted a huge flap of broken plywood and found Arthur, barely conscious. Her mother screamed, thinking he was dead, until his eyes flickered, then she cried and kissed his face. Tears ran down Lexi's cheeks— she hadn't killed her father after all.

The Senator yelled into her walkie-talkie to have an announcement made that any medical personnel left in the mall should report to the emergency medical center in the PaperClips on the first floor to assist with helping those hurt in the riot. Then her mother began hunting through the wreckage for supplies.

"Let me help," Lexi said, pushing herself to standing. Her legs still tingled, but they worked.

"Everything out here is trashed," Dotty said. "Let's get the stuff from the ICU."

She led Lexi toward the back of the PaperClips where a hole had been cut into the wall. A thick sheet of plastic hung over the opening.

"Wait here," her mother said. "We've been using this space to store the bodies we've found."

"How many have you found?" Lexi asked.

"So far, fifteen by my count."

"Sixteen," Lexi said. "A woman died in the Abercrombie."

Her mother's face softened. She pulled Lexi into a hug. "I'm sorry you had to see that," she said.

Lexi relaxed into her mother's arms, feeling like a weight had been lifted off her. She held tighter to her mother. "I'm so sorry I messed everything up," she said.

Her mother's breathing hiccupped; Lexi felt a tear against her cheek.

"Things were messed up from the beginning," Dotty said. "I'm sorry I got so angry."

The walkie-talkie crackled to life announcing that a doctor and two nurses had shown up at the front gate and were examining Arthur. Lexi and her mother unwound their arms. Looking at each other, they smiled.

"I should get those supplies," her mother said.

"I'll wait here," Lexi said.

Her mother kissed her forehead, then went through the plastic door. Lexi craned her neck to check what they were doing with her father. Then she heard her mother scream from inside the ICU.

Lexi swept the thick plastic aside and was greeted with a stench the likes of which not even the grossest garbage bin had achieved.

"Mom?" The foul air choked her voice. She pulled her shirt collar over her nose and mouth. She was inside the Pancake Palace, though it had changed drastically since her breakfast there last Sunday—it seemed like years had passed since then. Boxes marked "Medical Equipment" and "Freeze-Dried Food" lined what used to be the counter. The booths had been torn out and replaced by rows of shrouded gurneys, some covered in plastic tents.

The doors to the kitchen were still swinging. Lexi pushed through them and saw her mother standing in front of what must have been the walk-in freezer, her hand on the handle of the huge metal door.

"Don't come any closer," her mother said.

Lexi came closer.

A cold mist curled from the doorway. Frost glinted off something that, as the mist swirled, revealed itself to be a forehead.

Inside the freezer, in neat stacks, were bodies. Lexi counted twenty in the doorway alone.

"They told me only twenty had died." Her mother's voice was light, trembling. "Only twenty. There have to be fifty bodies in there."

Lexi guessed the number was higher.

"You can't tell anyone about this," her mother said, finally. She stepped forward, closing the door. "People will only panic if they know the flu is this serious."

"People are already panicking," Lexi said. How could her mother be talking about keeping more things secret? Hadn't she already seen the damage the last round of lies had caused?

"What would telling people accomplish?" her mother asked. "Run this through with me: We tell people that if they get sick, they're most likely going to die. Next, people will try to hide their symptoms, lie to themselves about being sick. This means they won't seek treatment, they'll stay out in the populace and infect more people."

"But you have to be honest with them," Lexi said.

"Honesty is not always the best policy." The Senator pulled the walkie-talkie from her belt. "I need a team in the ICU. Bring duct tape and caulk to seal a doorway."

Her mother walked into the kitchen, then noticed Lexi wasn't following.

"The team will take care of it," the Senator said. "Let's go check on your dad." She kept walking.

Lexi made a mental note of the space, projected the number of bodies inside. They were isolated in this mall for the foreseeable future and someone had to know the truth. Had to be ready with it for the next time the government decided to hide it with a deadly lie.

"Coming!" Lexi shouted, trotting to catch up.

And if that someone had to be her, then so freaking be it.

In the bright, clean, fresh air of the PaperClips, Lexi spotted her mother beside a gurney. In it rested her father, his arm bound between two strips of cardboard and held to his chest in a sling. His shirt had been cut away from his shoulder, which was wrapped in gauze.

"The Ross clan," he said. "Together again."

"Always," her mother said, smiling at Lexi.

"Always," Lexi said. And hoped it could be true.

THE SENATOR

Dotty folded the list and handed it to Hank, the waiting chief of security, a large cop who smelled like he hadn't even rinsed off since the beginning of this nightmare.

"You want me to make the announcement?" he said, perusing her work.

"No," she said, cranking her head forward until her neck cracked. "They know my voice now, I should do it." She took back the paper and stood. "You start the body search."

If there was a dead saleslady in the Abercrombie stockroom, there had to be others littered around the mall, and she wanted the corpses brought to the Pancake Palace before they caused any additional hysteria. She would distract the masses with her new plan to organize their mall society. Given the massive failure of the Feds' *lais-*

sez faire, live-wherever policy, she felt any plan was an improvement.

At least she had a handle on her family. Arthur was convalescing on the couch in the Apple Store stockroom and Lexi was sitting next to him helping to type in the population database she'd asked them to create. It was nice having all of the Rosses on the same page.

She made her way to the mall offices on the third floor, at the far end of the hall near the ice-skating rink. She'd been given the mall manager's access card after he fell ill. His was the first frozen face she'd recognized in the Pancake Palace freezer. It was a terrible thing to admit, but she would not miss his interfering presence.

The mall offices were empty save for the monitoring station. She and Hank had agreed that no matter what happened, they needed to keep one guard on the closed-circuit camera system. There were cameras covering every public space in the mall and the parking areas. These cameras were their eyes on the masses. It was through them that they'd had some warning of the oncoming riot and were able to evacuate the Feds and lock down the portal before anyone could escape and infect the world. That was the only order she'd been given by the president: Keep the virus from getting out.

This, of course, left the responsibility of managing a population—of several thousand—with her. She had four cops, one in a coma; a mall security force of fifty, a number that might be less after the bodies were finally identified; some hundred and fifty Tasers; four handguns, one of which was reported missing; two shotguns; ten canisters of tear gas; and twenty riot shields. This required not a little creative thinking.

She reached the microphone connected to the mall announcement system and collapsed into the chair beside it. She wiped the arm rests with a disinfecting cloth, then the mic itself, took a sip from her water bottle, and turned the system on.

"Attention, residents of the Shops at Stonecliff," she began. "I apologize for the manner in which yesterday's announcement was made. It was not our intention to cause anyone to panic. Anyone who suffered any injuries as a result of last night's incident should report to the medical center located in the PaperClips on the first floor. Anyone with any medical training should also please report to the PaperClips to assist in helping those injured.

"With respect to the flu virus announced yesterday, if you begin to develop symptoms, including chills, a cough, or a runny nose, please report to the PaperClips for treatment.

"Security guards will be handing out face masks and hand sanitizer. Please wear your mask and apply the sanitizer before touching any surface and before meals. Avoid touching your face. These small measures will help prevent the spread of the disease.

"We have been given additional cots by the government and will set these up in three locations within the mall. Families, please report to the HomeMart for registration and assignment of beds. Women and girls, please report to the JCPenney; men and boys, please report to the Lord and Taylor. These locations will be your Home Stores.

"If you are in need of a change of clothes, depots will be established on the first floor of each Home Store where you can trade in your clothes for a new set. You will no longer be able to purchase clothing. You will also not have a choice in what clothing you are given. We apologize in advance for any inconvenience this may cause.

"We have been given sufficient quantities of food by the government for the duration of this quarantine, however long it lasts. Meals will be served in the first-floor common areas. If you have a life-threatening food allergy, please notify the security guard when you register at your Home Store. Other than life-threatening conditions, we cannot accommodate any dietary requests.

"If you have any comments or concerns, please bring them to the attention of one of the security guards. We will try to address every situation to the best of our ability. This is an unusual and trying situation, but we are all in this together. By working together and following a few simple rules, we can all make it through this with the least incident and suffering. Thank you for you patience and attention. God bless you all."

She flipped off the machine and pushed the mic away. It was impossibly draining, infusing her voice with hope and energy to try to keep the masses from spiraling into despair. She just had to keep them hopeful. If they had hope, they could be controlled.

As she left the offices, she waved to the guard on duty— Ken, she thought; she had better learn their names—and stepped into the empty hall. This end of the third floor was always rather quiet, especially since the ice-skating rink was closed Thursday due to a coolant malfunction.

The senator glanced at the locked doors to the rink. *They couldn't have . . .*

She ran back into the offices. "Ken, where are the tenant keys?"

"Manager's office should have ones to a few stores, but we don't keep keys to the anchor stores."

"The ice-skating rink," she said. "I just need the key to that."

"That's one he should have," Ken said, leading her into the dark office once occupied by the odious little troll. "We're always having maintenance issues with that thing." Ken opened a cabinet and picked a small ring from a hook. "Here you go. You need to cool off?" he said, winking.

Dotty laughed because that was what you did when someone thought they were funny. *There should be Oscars for politicians.* She took the key and stalked out to the hall.

The doors to the skating rink opened into a dark vestibule. The temperature inside was several degrees colder. Dotty flicked on the lights. Pictures of smiling girls in spandex lined the walls. On one side of the foyer, there was a counter behind which rental skates gleamed; on the other, a dark office. In front of her were two more doors.

Dotty touched the handle of one and was shocked by the cold. The metal bit her fingertips. *Coolant failure, my ass . . .*

Slipping her hand inside her sleeve, she pushed the handle down and pulled open the door. A blast of freezing air slapped her skin. The rink was black as night—no light shined anywhere. Dotty felt around the inside of the doorway for a switch.

It took a minute for the lights strung high on the ceiling to reach full power, but even in their first dim glow, Dotty saw the bodies. They were piled on the ice. Row after row, not even wrapped in body bags. Arms splayed, hair falling over faces. The ice itself was tinged red.

Dotty's legs gave out. She slid against the door and came to rest on the frozen tile. There had to be hundreds on the ice. Maybe a thousand. This many couldn't have come through the med center—had these all been found in the mall or had patients died fast enough to keep pace with the newly sick? Was this why the Suits had refused to give her access to the intake logs at the PaperClips? *A thousand dead and they didn't tell me.*

But hadn't they? Why else would the president order a quarantine of thousands of citizens? Only if the virus was this deadly would the government have authorized trapping them like rats on a sinking ship.

She didn't have the luxury of panic. She pulled the walkie-talkie from its holster on her belt and clicked it to Hank's channel.

"New orders," she said.

"I'm listening."

"Bring the bodies to the ice-skating rink," she said. "Use the service passages. No civilians are to ever come into the skating rink."

"Roger that."

Had he known? He had to have known. How many people were harboring secrets from her? No more. She would canvass every goddamned inch of this mall before the end of the day. She would find that missing gun and nail those kids who blasted her cops with fire extinguishers and get things in some semblance of order before night fell. This was her sinking ship now. And Dorothy Ross ran a tight ship.

▪ END OF BOOK ONE ▪

ACKNOWLEDGMENTS

Thank you to my early readers, Anne Cunningham, Matt Weiner, Mary Beth McNulty, Alison Moncrief Bromage, Tui Sutherland, and my mom, Chris Kaufman—your comments helped me figure out the important stuff and your encouragement kept me going. Thank you, Brad Bergstresser, for your insights into online gaming. Thank you, Karen Mangold, for answering my endless questions and helping me kill more people more effectively. Thank you to my agent, Faye Bender, for believing in me and in this story. Thank you to my editor, Kathy Dawson, for being awesome, and to the whole team at Dial for making this dream a reality. And thank you to my wonderful husband for shouldering all the extra walkies and child care during the writing of this one, and thank you to my goat girl for being the best little girl in the whole wide world.